# A Long Day in Lychford

# ALSO BY PAUL CORNELL

# A LONG DAY
# IN LYCHFORD

## PAUL CORNELL

A TOM DOHERTY ASSOCIATES BOOK

NEW YORK

This is a work of fiction. All of the characters, organizations, and events portrayed in this novella are either products of the author's imagination or are used fictitiously.

A LONG DAY IN LYCHFORD

Cover photograph © Mark Owen/Arcangel
Cover design by FORT

Edited by Lee Harris

A Tor.com Book
Published by Tom Doherty Associates
175 Fifth Avenue
New York, NY 10010

www.tor.com

Tor® is a registered trademark of
Macmillan Publishing Group, LLC.

ISBN 978-0-7653-9317-3 (ebook)
ISBN 978-0-7653-9318-0 (trade paperback)

First Edition: October 2017

For Lizzie at 7a and Maxine at The Coffee Post
(the coffee shops of Fairford
where parts of this book were written)

# A Long Day in Lychford

# 1

Marcin Przybylski was lost, and the voice in the cab of his lorry wasn't being much help. "At the roundabout, take the third exit, and continue . . ."

He stared into the darkness of the tree-lined road ahead. "Where's the roundabout?" he asked his phone, helplessly. The phone was attached to a bracket on the dashboard, and illuminated as if to underline its importance. Because right now it ruled his life. Mr. Ofgarten, who right now would be asleep in his comfy bed, had some sort of beacon attached to each one of these phones. If, when he woke up and checked his enormous tablet over his delicious morning pastries, one of those drivers was not anywhere near, in this case, the brand new Tesco distribution centre at Pilning in Gloucestershire, however you were meant to pronounce that . . . well, there would be a stream of German obscenities down the line. It was said that to be more than twenty minutes late meant automatic dismissal. At least then Marcin could tell him what he could do with his smoked sausages.

He'd got to the Oxford distribution centre for Sainsbury's with no problem. That was second nature by now. It was the combination of this new location and this "brilliant new crowdsourced navigation app" that Ofgarten had installed that was foxing him.

A sign loomed ahead in the summer night. "Lychford," he said to the phone.

"I do not recognise the location," the phone replied.

"Of course not."

"I do not understand the instruction."

"Oh, go to hell!"

"Changing route now."

"No! Stop!"

"Stopping now." And the screen showed the moving circle that indicated it was waiting for further instructions.

Marcin managed to avoid bellowing at it, worried that might dig him in deeper. He was passing a new housing estate on the edge of this Lychford, woodlands on the other side. Was there anyone around here he could wake up at this time in the morning to ask for directions? How willing to answer their door would they be? And he didn't have much English. Did he trust his phone to translate for him?

Suddenly, the light seemed to change a little, and he jumped, worried that, despite being used to the night shift, he'd fallen asleep. But no. Still the woodlands. Maybe that had been lightning? Or was it getting light this early?

"Turn left," said his phone. Ah, it was back!

Only of course there didn't seem to be a . . . no, what was that up ahead? He couldn't see it properly, did he need glasses? The road seemed to suddenly—!

Marcin had to haul on the wheel as abruptly, impossibly, the road he was travelling on turned almost at a right angle and headed upwards into . . . what the hell was that?!

"I do not recognise this location!" yelled his phone. And it kept yelling it. As Marcin and his lorry skidded uncontrollably into what seemed like . . . nothingness.

———

Autumn Blunstone woke up, and gradually realised she was lying face down, fully clothed, in her own bed, upstairs at her magic shop, Witches, in the market town of Lychford, in the Cotswolds. These facts came to her one by one, introducing themselves politely.

The sun was already up. A cool breeze was ruffling the curtains. It was . . . really early still. Why was she awake?

Autumn felt . . . bloody awful. Not actually entirely . . . hungover, not yet. It was like the hangover was literally hanging over her, waiting to expand to its full dimensions, but had first just wanted to knock on her door to tell her it was getting ready to do its thing. We have a delivery for you, it was saying, and we will not hand it to a neighbour, but intend to unpack it in your every special place.

Knocking on her . . . no, someone was actually knocking on the door downstairs. Really quite loudly and urgently. At this time in the morning. And there was distant music somewhere out there. The *duff duff duff* of dance music. What was that about?

Autumn shouted something incoherent, reached out to find her robe, realised she didn't need to and fell out of bed.

———————

At the door she found PC Shaun Mawson, in uniform and definitely on business. In the air, from somewhere behind him, faded in and out that beat of some distant, ongoing rave.

"Miss Blunstone," he said, "can I come in? It's urgent." It must have been for him to call her by anything other than her first name, or more usually just a shy nod. Shaun was the son of Autumn's elderly employee and supposed mentor in the ways of magic, Judith, but he shared none of his mother's bloody-mindedness. Thank God. He turned down the offer of tea, and made Autumn sit down in the kitchen.

"Is someone . . . dead?" she asked.

"We don't know. That's why I'm here." He got out his notebook and pen and held up a hand to gently halt her questions. "Let's start at the beginning. Can you remember much about last night? Can you remember where you got to?"

Great question.

Worrying question.

Why *had* he asked her to sit down?

*No, come on, concentrate on the question.* Where *had* she been last night? Autumn had always said there was a pub in Lychford to suit her every mood. If you wanted the good company of builders and town councillors, there was the Plough. If you wanted to meet people who were just passing through, or to sit and read quietly, there was the Market Hotel. If you wanted noise, youth, and the offer of drugs in the toilets, there was the Randolph. And if you wanted a fight, there was the Custom House. That was it for the pubs of Lychford these days. A couple had closed down recently. When Autumn had been a teenager, there'd been seventeen. Over the years, her range of options had narrowed, but, neatly, so had her range of moods.

"I think I was at . . . the Custom House?"

The Custom House was the sort of pub that the town council kept wanting to find a good reason to close down. The dusty whitewash on the outside gave one a clue that here was an inn the carpet of which could have been the subject of a TV nature special by David Attenborough. As you headed for the bar, your footsteps crunched. The walls inside were bare, the cloth on the pool table ripped, though people still played on it. The fruit machine's soundboard had once had a pint tipped into it, resulting in strange, muffled, warblings. However, the landlord, Malcolm, kept the beer pipes clean, and for the Custom House's clientele, that was the only required saving grace. After you got to know people, the décor became a feature, not a bug.

But yeah, there were often fights.

"Why did you decide to go there?" Shaun's tone suggested that no nice young lady would. Autumn tended to end up at the Custom House having had a couple of drinks at one of the other pubs, become slightly angry with something someone had said there—but not enough to want to cause a fuss—and thus decided to move on. Her light complexion, what her best friend Lizzie had once called her "had clothes fall on her accidentally" sense of style, and, she supposed, the fact that she'd always been around, all distracted from the fact that she was, as they said these days, a person of colour. So she overheard things in those other pubs: perfectly nice people who'd never use the N word still saying "chinky" and, incredibly, "pikey"; people on her own social level knowing they were being risqué when they'd had a few, making jokes that started with "Jewboy and Mick walk into a pub." When she'd been younger, she'd always spoken up at that point, and had been pleased when there'd often been whoops of applause rather than dismissal. Some of it was "oh ah, here she goes again," but some of it had always been that feeling that she was to be congratulated for speaking up for "her own people." Not that she knew, apart from her extended family in Swindon, any of her own people. Not since her Dad had passed away. She was literally the only non-white person in the entire town. That, she suspected, was the only circumstance in which you'd get that welcoming reaction, when the majority thought of you as the sole representative, and therefore harmless. Of course, in Lychford, there were also Sunil Mehra and his employees, but she'd never felt they had much in common. Sunil was part of the "reception for the Prince of Wales" crowd in this town, who'd probably see himself as "one of them," while she was . . . whatever class it was that owned magic shops.

She was aware that, as she'd gotten older and still overheard things in pubs, she'd stopped speaking up so much.

Because when you stopped being a teenager, you started feeling less sure of yourself, and not everything seemed like it was life and death. And she liked fitting in. She was quite popular, wasn't she? And these were good people, really. Really. But it hadn't eased off like she used to think it was going to. It had gotten worse. It had gotten more normal. The ones being "risqué" seemed to find it easier to say.

And then last year, that bloody year.

The walk through the marketplace on the day after the Brexit vote had been like something out of a science fiction movie. And that was saying something, coming from someone who was getting used to seeing magical beings. Which of these people, she had thought, looking around herself on that market day, had voted to saw themselves off from the rest of Europe? Which of these people, in their heart of hearts, wanted a Lychford that was "just like it had been in the 1950s"? Which of the shops she spent money in were owned by people who wanted the full emulsion white paint job, corner to corner, maybe without even having thought about it enough to know that was what they wanted? Which of the coffee shops contained people who were cheering inside today? She'd never know, because this was Britain, after all, and nice people don't talk about anything that might cause trouble, and so all that day the town had been weirdly silent.

She'd gone down the pub that night, and people hadn't talked about it there, either, but Autumn had overheard things, a lot of things, and that had been the first time she'd found herself going down the road to the Custom House. In the weeks and months that had followed, she'd found herself going there more and more. And now the General Election was approaching. And she felt more worried and scared every day. She'd talked with Lizzie about how she felt, and that always made her feel better for a while, like going on the Women's March in Bristol after Trump's election had made her feel better for a while. But the trouble with talking about this with Lizzie was that Lizzie would never understand how much these things made Autumn feel like an outsider in her own town. It had been months now, and she still couldn't find a way to haul herself out of the pit that social media dropped her into every morning. She looked at the future, and for the first time in her life, the way ahead looked uniformly grim. There were such incredible things in people's lives now, like photos from space probes around Saturn, and such incredible things outside those lives, the magic only the three of them knew about, and yet still, still, these tiny bloody people with their pent-up little bloody fears—! Even if she could have put it all into words, she couldn't be sure Shaun Mawson would ever understand.

"I don't know," she said. "I don't know why I went to the Custom House."

"Did anything . . . particularly stressful happen to you yesterday? I'm wondering how worked up you were when you got there."

Yesterday had been a long, sweaty summer day, which had seemed to gather up anger within itself, ready for a storm. And, oh God . . . yeah, she remembered now, the storm had broken. During that day, she had ended up having the row she was always going to have. And, horribly, it had been with the mother of the police officer who was facing her now. It had been with Judith.

They'd fallen into it by accident. The old witch of the hedgerow, as Judith liked to style herself, both mentally and in terms of grooming, had sat permanently behind the till that day, just like most days now, glaring at any tourists who might happen to come into the shop, setting quizzes about the occult history of Gloucestershire in the sixteenth century to any of them who might offhandedly try to strike up a conversation about crystals or the healing energy of unicorns. It was like Autumn was keeping a troll behind the counter, in every sense of the word. She had wondered hopefully, in the last few months, as Judith's attitude to people had got worse, if Judith might seem like the more challenging end of the real ale spectrum, that people might start to say that was the real thing at that magic shop, that, horrible as it tasted, it was the genuine experience. But no, after the third tourist yesterday had left without buying anything, at a speed which left the shop bell bashing against its hanger, Autumn had finally dropped the idea of monetising the degree of difficulty her employee presented to the world. "Okay," she'd said, "you can't keep doing that. What with Brexit, I need to start making some sales here—"

"What about it?"

Autumn had realised that, at the end of a tiring day, she had finally let slip what she had avoided talking about with Judith all this time. She had said the magic word. Ironically. Still, she knew that Judith's grasp of economics was usually that of an elderly aunt who every year tried to bet five pence each way on the Grand National.

"Any supplies I get in from Europe are now literally worth their weight in gold, and given everything that's happened this year, the council will be putting the rates up."

Judith had made a dismissive sound in her throat. "Things'll get better."

Autumn had paused, wondering if that had meant what she'd thought it had. Judith had made grudging eye contact, then looked away. And Autumn had recalled how, according to the polls, there had been a direct correlation between one's closeness to the cemetery and how willing one was to mess up the future for generations to come. It had occurred to her that it would be just like Judith to have done what a number of the folk down the pub seemed to have done: to have taken any yes/no question from any government as an immediate reason to burn down their own house and everyone else's. "Okay, you got me. You've been working hard today to separate my shop from its customers. I'm interested in how you feel about separating other stuff. Which way did you vote?"

Judith had glared at her. "None of your business."

Which nobody on the Remain side ever said. It was only the Leavers who wanted to hide it. "Oh no. You did, didn't you?"

"Vote's private. That's democracy, isn't it?"

"But you're not proud of it?"

"I don't talk about politics or religion."

"You're a *witch*, who works in a *magic shop* and, like the car sticker would say, your other apprentice is a *vicar*."

"I don't talk about politics. Stop going on. Do you want a cuppa?"

Which had been the first time in the history of their association that Judith had ever offered to make the tea. The enormity of this distraction might even have worked, if Autumn had been willing to let it. With the sun getting lower in the shop window, the row might have faded and

Autumn might have decided to let it go, let her go, let her go back to her house and annoy her neighbours instead. As the song so nearly put it. But that had been the moment, Autumn remembered now, the moment she'd realised something huge about the situation she and Lizzie were in, something that had felt in that second like sheer complicity on her part. "Oh my God," she said. "That's what you're teaching us to do."

"What?" Judith had looked at Autumn like she'd gone mad.

"We're *defending the borders* of this town. We're here to *deter the outsiders*. That's what we're all about, isn't it? That's what we *do*."

There had been a long silence. There had been, even then, Autumn thought now, things Judith could have said.

But instead, Judith had slowly got to her feet. "Do you want me to keep on working here, then?" Those merciless old eyes had fixed on Autumn. Judith had done what she always did. She had boiled down the complexities of a situation to some ridiculous basics.

Autumn had wanted to say of course she wanted Judith to stay. She really had. But in the heat of that moment, she hadn't been able to get the words out. Instead, she'd said nothing.

After a moment, Judith had picked up her bag from

under the desk, and headed for the door. Autumn had wanted to call to her before she got there. She had not.

So Judith had left, and the door had closed gently behind her.

It had taken Autumn a few minutes after Judith had left to move at all.

When she had, it had been fast. She had been shaking with emotion. She had locked up the till, locked up the shop, slammed the bolts . . . and headed down to the Custom House.

"It had just . . . been a long day," she said to Shaun now. "I'd had some problems with one of my staff."

He carefully wrote that down. What was going on here? She felt like she'd just somehow incriminated herself. "Okay," he said. "Was there any trouble when you were in the pub itself?"

Autumn recalled that she hadn't been the first to set forth across the crunchy carpet of the Custom House last night. Her heart had sunk, in fact, when she'd seen who'd gotten there before her for early doors. It had been Jenker. Keith Jenkins, he was properly called, a taxi driver who'd married someone in the Backs. The Custom House was his local. Earlier that summer, when Autumn had come in complaining about the heat, he'd said something about her working on her suntan. At the time, she hadn't been quite sure whether or not he'd meant it lit-

erally, and he'd maintained eye contact, kept that inno-
cent grin on his ruddy, aye aye, here's the life and soul of
the party face. She couldn't help but be wary of him after
that, though, and yeah, she'd overheard things.

"Hello hello!" he'd boomed yesterday night. "Here
comes trouble."

Which would normally have been the sort of greeting
she loved. But not from him. And especially not after the
day she'd had. She'd nodded to him, she remembered,
and ordered a pint of 6B. It would have been impossible,
in the circumstances, not to talk to him, but the last thing
she'd wanted to talk about was what had happened with
Judith and the guilt and anger that were wrestling within
her. He'd tried the normal, harmless, topics, such as foot-
ball and the weather, and she'd nodded along, barely listening to his replies. With anyone else, on any other day,
she would gleefully have raised the subject of the weird-
ness of her work at the magic shop. She liked to present
what she did, at least the public part of it, to her pub
friends in all its eccentricity and have them tease her
about it. But she couldn't do that with Jenker. She
wouldn't make herself sociably vulnerable to him.

After a couple of drinks, however, she'd taken something he said for a starting point for a conversation that
swiftly turned into come on, did he feel okay with how
things were now, when you couldn't say anything on

Twitter without some fascist, some, I mean, literal fascist, someone who if you asked "are there any fascists here?" would put up his hand and say "actually . . ."? It had turned out Jenker wasn't on Twitter, and thought people who paid too much attention to the Internet were a bit . . . he'd made big boggly eyes at her.

Where had it gone from there? Oh God, she was starting to remember. Shaun the police officer was actually quite good at this interviewing thing, wasn't he?

After three drinks, one of which Jenker had bought her, and she'd suddenly started to wonder if he thought she was coming on to him, but no, that moment had gone past without comment, they'd started to seriously argue about what Brexit was going to mean to the economic future of Britain. He kept cutting her off and saying "nah," while making points she found she didn't have the information to hand to come back about. If you were a "crap farmer, not a good farmer," you had reason to vote to stay in, he said, but fishermen had a good reason to vote out. Then Autumn said what about wanting to keep all the brown people out, and he'd said it wasn't about the brown people, he was mates with a lot of brown people, like her, no offence, it was the bloody Poles and the whatever they were from central Europe, who couldn't speak English, taking their jobs, bringing their own shops over here and their foreign muck into our supermarkets. If she thought it was about brown people, that was where the chip on her shoulder had come from. No offence. Here, Autumn had been on steadier ground, at least in terms of data, and she'd held her own, and had actually said out loud that she felt she was one of *those* people too. *Every* sort of those people. He'd said, what you? You've been here longer than I have! He'd started holding up a finger for his interruptions, and had said they should have another pint and blimey love, you can talk, can't you, you and me must have been separated at birth, maybe I had a touch of the tar brush too, 'cos you're not full on, are you, you're half and half, so I don't see what you've got to worry about, and she'd been about to . . . explode? Yeah, hopefully she'd been about to do that rather than force a laugh, when one of the many, many people who had somehow filled the pub around them, some of whom were now looking on in glee or embarrassment, had spoken up.

*Oh. Oh my God.* She remembered now.

This was him. She remembered his face. An old lad, in his seventies, newspaper under his arm. A ruddy, drinker's face, balding, a fleck of grey stubble on his chin. He was so important. Why was he so important? What had happened to him?

"There . . . wasn't really any trouble," she said to Shaun. "Bit of a row."

"Do you remember anyone in particular being there?"

She mentioned Jenker. But okay, Shaun probably had in mind this . . . weirdly important guy she'd just remembered. "Someone told me his name was . . . Old Rory?"

"Rory Holt." That seemed to be the box he'd been wondering if she was going to tick. "Did he say anything in particular to you?"

Yeah. Yeah, he had, now Shaun had made her think of it. And it had been a terrible thing. It would have appeared in her memory, sometime today. It would have popped up, to bring her crashing down. Like it had halted her in her tracks now.

She could see him in her mind's eye now, a little grin on his face as he'd said it. "Bloody good idea." That's what he'd said.

"What is?" she'd replied.

"A wall," he'd said. "Trump's got it right. We should build one too. Keep 'em all out."

Which had gotten laughs, because come on this was still Britain, and nobody, whatever their politics, flew a flag for the most ridiculous American of them all, and that had come out of bloody nowhere. But it had left Autumn speechless. It had been a one-two punch with the awkward anger at what Jenker had just said.

She had stared at the old man. He'd met her gaze, challenging her. He hadn't looked away. His gaze said, *What the hell are you doing here in my sight? Did you think we were equal? This is my home. Not yours.*

Jenker had tapped her on the shoulder. "Old Rory's been reading the Internet too much," he'd said, and made the boggly eyes again. "Do you want another?"

Was that how furious the look on her face had been, that he'd felt he'd needed to distract her?

What had happened next? She remembered leaving the pub . . . didn't she? Had that been soon after? Had she had that next drink and lost track? Had she lost track of Rory Holt too?

"What happened next?" asked Shaun.

"I . . . I really don't know. Could you tell me why you're asking me all this?"

Shaun pursed his lips.

---

Like a lot of elderly people, Judith Mawson didn't need much sleep, and thus tended to get up early. She would put the television on in her kitchen and watch something stupid before the news as she made a very early breakfast, these days usually consisting of whatever half-arsed cereal the doctor said she needed to force down for the sake of her . . . heart, usually, but pick any organ. Like they said, eating healthy food might not help you live longer, but it certainly made you feel like you were. In the last six months or so, as she went through her usual ritual, she'd find herself glancing at the stairs, always thinking she'd heard a voice, when actually she hadn't.

"Stupid," she whispered to herself. "Soft."

Judith had got used to living with the spiteful ghost of Arthur, her husband, or rather, a curse that had taken his shape. The spectre might have been evil and cruel, but at least he'd been company. She was still trying to find a way to deal with the lack of another presence in the house, and thus, for the first time, having to completely accept that the real Arthur was gone. It was a strange, attenuated sort of grieving, made worse by Judith only having two people she could talk about it with: her apprentices, Autumn and Lizzie. Well, make that one person, after yesterday. The thought of it made her stop, with the cereal packet in mid-air. She had to take a moment to control her anger, as she had so many times before finally getting to sleep last night. Of course that stupid girl had wanted her to stay on at the shop, she just hadn't been able to bring herself to say the words. And that wasn't bloody good enough. Before she set foot in that place again, before she let Autumn resume her training, she would want, at the very least, an apology. And more money. And . . . whatever bloody else that stupid, stupid—!

Judith stopped herself. Her doctor probably wouldn't approve of her getting so worked up, and what for? It had only been the sort of thing young folk did, with their emotions flooding all over the place like spilt milk. She'd lost sleep about it, but so what? She wouldn't go in today, get an afternoon nap, let the stupid girl come to her.

For the umpteenth time, she put that matter to the back of her mind. What was worrying her more right now was this note she'd found attached to her fridge by a magnet. It made no sense. The note said:

*Remember that your parents are dead, you great fool.*

Which was ridiculous, because Judith's parents still lived next door like they'd always done. Only . . . no, that wasn't true, was it? She clicked her tongue, annoyed with herself. That was her getting old. Joyce who had that horrible laugh lived there now, with her parakeet. So . . . Judith's parents must have moved out, but . . . they'd have told her where they were going, wouldn't they?

They must have moved out.

Where?

This bloody note, making no sense. Nothing of magic about it, either. It hadn't just appeared. Someone had, quite normally, written it and put it there.

The weirdest thing about the note was, it was in Judith's own handwriting.

---

The Reverend Lizzie Blackmore groaned, and threw out a hand to hit her clock radio. It was only when her hand had connected three times to the button atop the radio, and she had only succeeded in switching it on, and it had filled the room with the soothing really very early morning sounds of BBC Radio 2, that she realised it was not actually 6:30 a.m., but a whole hour earlier. She switched it off, and then realised what had actually awoken her. The sound of distant music was wafting through her open window. *Duff, duff, duff,* dance music, so far away you could only hear the beat, then the beat changing, then back to the previous beat. She got up, stumbled to the window, and closed it. That wouldn't be uncomfortable. The Vicarage was cool in summer, if bloody freezing in winter. But she could still hear the beat, like a distant tapping. It was locked into her consciousness, specific and now just at the volume that made your ears listen out for it. Had it stopped? No, there it was. Had it stopped now? Nope.

She went back to bed and listened for about ten minutes to the changing beat, without wanting to. If it would only stay the same for a minute or two, she could have fallen asleep to it. She really didn't feel much like bloody dancing. Finally, she got up, put on her dressing gown, and grabbed from her bedside table the item which was now ruling her life. She'd gotten the Exercise Tracker for herself as a New Year's present, following that rather traumatic Christmas. The little electronic sadist was already making a bit of a difference to the size of her arse. Then she headed for the stairs, intending to make a cup of tea. She could spend this extra hour sending out a few emails, getting ahead of the day's problems. And perhaps she could play *Overwatch* for a bit.

She was surprised, and then alarmed, as she walked blearily down the stairs, to hear that the kettle was already boiling. She stopped, remembering that the burglar alarm was still below her in the hall. It was only relatively recently, after she'd been bathed in the water from the well in the woods, and become able to see the magical powers surrounding and threatening Lychford, that she'd even started turning it on. She couldn't get to the emergency button, but her phone was charging upstairs. She'd started to carefully make her way back up when a voice called from below. "Do you want a cuppa?"

She recognised the voice, and the way it had just said the most ordinary of sentences as if it was learning a foreign language, and was first relieved, then angry.

She marched down the stairs and into the kitchen to

find Finn, Prince of the Fairies, appreciatively watching her kettle boil as if it was some sort of modern art installation. "What the hell are you doing here?" she said.

He turned to look at her, not his usual jovial self. "Something strange is happening. I'd have gone to see, you know, the other one—"

"You mean Autumn? Your ex?"

Finn's supernaturally handsome features creased into the most gorgeous frown Lizzie had ever seen. It really was hard to stay angry with him. Which was, in itself, worrying. "I can't be expected to remember everyone. You people keep . . . reproducing. And then I look up from whatever I'm doing and you've had a millennium and I'm like 'where *does* the time go?' and—"

"Is there any point in asking how you got in? And yes, now you're here, I do want some strong black coffee, thank you."

Finn, as if he was following the most exotic process of preparation, and looking to her for guidance every other moment, made just that, and for himself poured hot water onto a tea bag it looked like he'd brought along, because Lizzie was pretty sure she didn't own any that glowed green. "I got in by walking down past the walls, which was really hard, as expected, because the Vicarage still has about it some of the old shapes of protection."

"I thought that in Lychford the vicar and, you know,

magic people were always on the same side?"

Finn took a long drink from his mug, and glowed slightly green himself for a moment. "You church folk are indeed usually allies with the wise woman of the town, but the nation of my father, we're not always friends with humans. This is reasonably easy to grasp, surely? Human beings still have different nations. You have borders even from your allies, right?"

"True."

"So those who built the Vicarage made its shape to defend against people like me slipping in and out without a lot of effort. Hence this." He pointed to his mug. "Keeps my strength up. Like I said, I'd have gone to see one of the other two for preference, but the old one's got some serious 'keep away' hoo-hah round her place these days, and Autumn's got a guest over."

"Oh?" Lizzie realised she'd put the wrong note in her voice and changed it to a more neutral "Oh."

Finn raised a frankly delightful eyebrow. "How *are* she and that new lad of hers doing?"

"How do you know about that?"

Finn just pointed at himself.

"Has that question got anything to do with the sort of company she's got this morning?"

"Not sure. Probably not. So how *are* she and Luke doing?"

Lizzie noted that he knew Autumn's boyfriend's name. "They have their ups and downs, but they're still together. He's off on some teaching thing up north."

"Probably for the best."

"Why?"

"Because of this strangeness that's been going on. As I was about to say before I was so rudely interrupted, today it wasn't just the shape of this place that made it hard to get in here. Something has happened to the borders. Leaving fairy and getting into Lychford is normally just about taking a step here and a step there. This time it was like stumbling down a hill. I felt like I'd crash any moment, and I don't know what crashing would even involve. When I get back, everyone'll be yelling about this."

"That is worrying. Okay, thanks for—"

"But that's not why I came here! I only found that out on the way here! And now I think of it, maybe the two are connected, because this is damnable, this is unconscionable, this I was sent from the court of my father with urgent diplomatic condemnation concerning!"

Lizzie held up her hands, amazed at the sudden fury which had taken him over. It was as if he had remembered that he was supposed to be officially angry, and in that moment, took on that emotion for real. Once again, she'd been reminded that though a fairy like Finn might

resemble a human being, he was actually very different.
"What?!"

"*What*," yelled Finn, pointing out of the window in the
direction of the repetitive beats, "is that bloody *music*?"

Lizzie could only shrug in agreement. "I know." Then
she realised she was representing possibly the entire human race in an official diplomatic negotiation with
another . . . species? If that was what fairies were. Not
a situation she expected to encounter while still in her
dressing gown. She made herself straighten up and ad-
justed her robe. "I mean . . ." she said, more carefully, "I
don't know."

Finn sighed. "I now have a new winner for our 'stupid
things humans say' board."

"Do you really have a—?"

"What you're trying to say is: *you* don't know what
that music is either?"

"I know *what* it is." And before he could scream in frustration, Lizzie quickly explained the concept of illegal
raves, from the perspective of someone who'd last gone
out dancing two decades ago.

Finn seemed relieved to at least have an explanation
he could take back to his father. "Well, normally I'd be all
for that, and good work there with the mind-expanding
drugs, because at least someone here's *trying*, but how is
the sound of it getting into fairy? We've got stuff to do,

you know. We need the sleep of ages under the hills. We can't be having with *dush dush dush* all the time."

"So the dance music is . . . keeping the fairies awake?"

"That's what I just said. Try to keep up."

"Well, our local police, such as they are, will be out trying to find it, I should think."

"Probably, though I've seen a few of them this morning doing other things besides. But what worries me most is, since I got here I've had a bit of a look for where the music's coming from, and I can't find it. And I have the nose of a bloodhound. In my pocket." He took something that Lizzie really hoped was a felt novelty of some kind from his jacket and showed it to her. "So your police won't be able to. You put that together with the borders getting messed up, and it's big trouble for everyone."

"You're right. I'll tell the others."

Finn seemed satisfied. "Excellent. This is what the three of you are for." He threw back the remains of his tea, then glanced suspiciously at Lizzie, carefully washed out his mug, and retrieved the tea bag. "Good luck with it. Now I have to go home and listen to everyone at court getting worked up all over again. Let's hope you can deal with it before that boils over into, you know, the collapse of reality. Or whatever." And with a gesture that seemed somehow dismissive as well as functional, he vanished. Then there was a sudden *clonk* sound from somewhere inside the walls, and a cry of pain, and then a motion of air that Lizzie somehow knew meant that now he'd actually gone, on the second attempt, and that the Vicarage's old defences were still good for some things.

Lizzie's first impulse was to go and see what sort of company Autumn had at this time in the morning, but no, Judith was who she should go to find.

She went back upstairs, pleased at having added an unexpected flight of steps to her fitness tracker's records, dressed, then headed off to Judith's house.

As she walked up the hill from the marketplace, that distant sound of dance music was still drifting over the town. It was indeed weird that, if that was an illegal rave, the police hadn't found it and closed it down by now. Something that loud couldn't be legal, could it? Wouldn't she have had a warning letter through her door, or something?

There didn't initially seem to be anyone at home at Judith's house. But that was often the case these days. Lizzie knew Judith had been grieving in a manner that was, quite possibly, unique in all of human history. Lizzie had been doing her best to help, because comforting grieving widows was very much part of her skill set, but Judith had been, as expected, one of her more challenging subjects. The old lady's desire to not say anything to anyone about anything unless it was somehow offensive had reached a new intensity in these last few months. It took a bit of work for anyone dealing with her to realise that she'd changed, because she now bore an entirely different burden than the one she'd borne for years before. And that burden had been made worse, of course, by its own potential for change, that someday Judith might bear no burden at all. The weight on her shoulders had grown to be part of her, had informed the malice that often seemed, to those who didn't know her well, to be what kept her going.

At Lizzie's third ring of the bell, the door opened. Judith stood there, looking even more grim than usual. "I was just about to come and find you," she said. "Summat terrible has happened."

"I know—" began Lizzie.

"No you don't," said Judith.

———

"We're dealing with two missing persons cases this morning," Shaun had said, when Autumn had pressed him for details. "We think you might have particular insight into one of them. Rory Holt is missing."

"Oh no." Autumn had felt a horrible tension building in her stomach. She'd tried to keep her expression steady.

But Shaun had looked at her as if that reaction had

been meaningful. "His daughter, who lives with him, called it in in the early hours. She thought she'd heard him arrive home, but when she got up to go to the bathroom, the door to his room was open and his bed hadn't been slept in. He was nowhere in the house. She thinks he must have actually gone missing between leaving the pub and getting to their doorstep. Right now, we think you were the last person to see him."

"Why do you think that?"

"Because there's security camera footage of you two . . . continuing your altercation."

"You got to see security camera footage this early in the morning?"

Shaun had sighed. "I do sometimes wish the public didn't watch so many detective shows. We saw it because it was from the security camera on the front of the police station."

Autumn had indeed watched her share of police procedurals, and had thus suddenly been very aware of what this meant. She'd been the last to see the victim . . . and she'd been arguing with him. "You're saying I'm some sort of . . . suspect."

Shaun had looked awkward. "A Detective Inspector's coming up from Swindon, about both cases. The brass are wondering if they've somehow got anything to do with the illegal rave that's been reported. We were told to go out and interview everyone who might be . . . involved." A buzz had come from his phone and he'd looked at it, then looked up. "She's here now, and I'm to ask you if you'll come in for interview."

Which was how Autumn now found herself inside Lychford police station, waiting to be interviewed. She'd immediately taken up the offer to have legal representation present. The solicitor in question seemed businesslike, a little remote. Autumn numbly listened as she'd filled her in on the basics of what was going to happen. She'd never been inside Lychford police station before. It was seldom open these days, a tiny adjunct to the trading estate. Now it had a cluster of police cars and vans in front of it, and there had even been a reporter from a local radio station, with a power pack, a microphone, and a look on his face which said this was the biggest thing with which he'd ever been involved.

Shaun had sighed again as they'd made their way across the car park. "More of those'll be on the way." He was looking at her, Autumn had realised, like she'd let him down, like she was part of his world which wasn't behaving as he wanted it to. Most coppers knew, from long experience, she remembered reading, that the obvious suspect had usually done it.

The reporter had seen Autumn and moved quickly, had taken a picture. She'd been caught staring, she realised, wondering if trying to get a hand in the way would make the image look worse to whatever friends and relations might see it.

She'd been given a cup of black coffee, which had been welcome, and left in this interview room with the solicitor. The guilt and the anger and the hangover were now all one thing. Oh God, she should have called Lizzie. She should have called Luke. She was remembering more and more now. And it was all bad.

A female plainclothes police officer entered, with, again, that look of businesslike distance about her, and introduced herself as D.I. Pearce. She began with some legal formalities Autumn really didn't like the sound of, telling her she was going to be recording the interview. Then she started the tape decks running. Pearce led her through the same chain of events Shaun had, referring to his notes on occasion. She kept it so by the book that Autumn's solicitor kept nodding along. Autumn felt, horribly, like the two of them were workers in an industrial process and she was their raw material. She said the minimum, agreeing with her previous version of events. Then they got to the point to which Shaun had taken the narrative. "When you left the pub, where was Rory Holt?"

"He followed me. He was shouting at me."

"What was he saying?"

She could remember every detail now. "He was

using ... you know ... hate speech."

"What *exactly*?"

So Autumn was forced to put those words in her mouth. They made her feel sick all over again. To voice them felt like she was being made to bully herself. She watched the face of the D.I. for any sign of sympathy, but she remained utterly neutral. Autumn talked as, moment by moment, the memory unfolded in front of her, of how Old Rory had pushed past her and so, yes, damn it, she'd followed him, up past the police station, with him turning to spit on the ground and yell back at her.

"Just past the police station, I yelled at him one last time, and I thought ... this sounds so stupid now ... I thought yeah, that showed him. I turned around and walked off, talking loudly so I ... couldn't hear what else he was saying. Like I said, stupid. I ... must have gone back the other way, not past that camera again."

She looked into Pearce's eyes, hoping to see some sign that she believed what Autumn now was pretty certain was the truth. No response.

There was a knock on the door, and Pearce called to enter. A uniformed officer came in and whispered something to her. Pearce seemed to gain a certain tension across her shoulders. She excused herself, and left, leaving the recorders on. The solicitor said that some new development must have occurred, as if that wasn't obvious. Autumn was barely listening, she was so relieved at having found this exonerating memory, so giddy with that release.

So why did she still feel guilty, somewhere at the back of her mind?

It was the hangover. It must be. And, okay, yelling in the street at a pensioner, even at a racist pensioner, perhaps not her finest hour. And she could never feel certain that the police would agree with her newfound proof of innocence.

After half an hour, Pearce returned. She asked a couple more questions of a general nature, and wrote down her contact details, at which point Autumn realised she was actually going to . . . not get away with this, where had that thought come from? To justifiably be let off the hook. Her solicitor broke into a smile that seemed to be about this taking less time than she thought it would.

Autumn stumbled out of the interview room, trying to restrain her trembling. In the reception area, she found Shaun, who now looked a little guilty himself. He gave her a significant look, waited until another copper had walked past, then moved close enough to whisper to her. "Just doing our job, you know."

"It's okay." Because now she was in a mood to be charitable, and he'd been fine, honestly. He couldn't help . . . unconsciously condemning her. *No, stop thinking like that, Autumn.*

"Turns out an old lady called it in. You woke her up. She saw you walk off just like you said you did, and saw Rory go the other way. And bless her, she stayed awake and kept watching."

"Oh thank God."

"She was afraid for him, and thought from what you'd been yelling that you might go back after him."

It took Autumn a moment to process that. "From what *I'd* been yelling?! Didn't she hear what *he* was—?!"

"It's not me saying this."

"No, no you're right. Sorry. Hey, you said two missing persons. Who's the other?"

"A lorry driver. The transponder on his vehicle said he'd swerved off the road, then it stopped working. Which is often a sign the rig's been hijacked. Hard to see how it all fits together. I suppose it's possible that three different illegal things this big have happened at once by coincidence. But that'd be three times more than we've ever had in any given year. Still. Maybe times are changing." That beaten down look had returned to his face. At least now it wasn't about her.

"Thanks, Shaun. Listen, if you see your Mum—"

"What?"

Autumn paused. No, maybe not. That was something she should do herself. If she was going to do it at all.

———————

Lizzie had been looking open-mouthed between what was on Judith's kitchen floor and Judith herself, as the old witch had told her what it meant. Then she'd had to have a sit down, and Judith had told her where to find the tea to make herself a cup. "We'll need to wait a while before the stupid girl can get here," she'd said.

'Where is she now? And don't call her—"

"In the circumstances," Judith had muttered, "I intend to call her a lot more than that."

Lizzie had spent the next hour or so walking up and down the kitchen, avoiding the pool of liquid, worrying and checking the step count on her wrist. Finally, the doorbell rang.

It was indeed Autumn, who entered with her hands above her head, exclaiming, "You would not believe the morning I've had."

"We would," said Judith. "Look." And she pointed at the floor.

Autumn stopped and stared too.

On the usually spotless kitchen floor, as Lizzie had discovered when she first got here, was a pool of water, only it was reflecting the sunlight more brightly than ordinary water would. Judith poked the pool with the toe of her fluffy slipper. It rippled, and on its surface suddenly appeared a frozen image of Autumn outside the police station.

Autumn closed her eyes. "You have no right to—"

"Let's not start about who's got the right to do what," said Judith sharply. "More important, there's this." She picked up a washing-up liquid bottle from her sink and squeezed something onto the surface of the pool. The picture changed.

Lizzie was once again looking at the image Judith had shown her before. It was the wall of someone else's kitchen. On it was a wobbling red circle, like a heat haze made flesh. "Only we can see that," Lizzie explained to Autumn.

"Where is this?"

"Don't you recognise it?" asked Judith.

Autumn was frowning, deeply upset. "No," she finally whispered.

"What about this?" Judith kicked the image and it swung round to reveal the black silhouette of a person, with limbs flailing in all directions, that was embedded in the opposite wall.

"And only we can see that too—" Lizzie began.

Autumn cut her off. "I don't need a running commentary. Where *is* this?"

"I think," growled Judith, "you two had better come with me."

———————

Autumn walked briskly beside Judith as they headed to her shop. She didn't want to think; she didn't want to let her memory go where it wanted to. That kitchen in the picture had seemed horribly familiar, and she was starting to realise . . . oh God no, it couldn't be true. That distant music was still beating away, meaninglessly.

She unlocked the door of the shop and the three of them went inside, Lizzie with that terrible calm on her face that she reserved for the ordinary horrors that vicars encountered. She kept trying to make reassuring eye contact, but Autumn couldn't bring herself to accept that comfort. Judith led them through toward the back room, the workroom.

The smell hit her as they approached. The smell from what was inside.

And Autumn started to remember the last time she'd come here.

She rushed toward the door to her lab. She had to get there first. She flung it open.

She fell against the wall inside, coughing.

The stench was overpowering. In the past, Judith had worked on the rest of the shop so that the smells in here wouldn't escape to where the customers were, or rather, to where her own nose usually was. Ingredients bags and boxes were lying open all around. Autumn saw that some of what was causing the smell was still bubbling on a pot by the sink.

Judith went over to it, looked at it like it was the enemy, picked up a pan lid with the corner of her cardigan, and slammed it down on the pot. She looked to switch off the heat, then realised at the same moment Autumn did that the cooker wasn't actually on. "That'll need cleaning," she said. "Cleaning with the proper stuff." Meaning, Autumn realised, stuff that wasn't to be found in any mundane kitchen cupboard.

Lizzie went to the pot, made the sign of the cross, closed her eyes, and mouthed some words. She opened them again and saw Autumn looking hopelessly at her. "Couldn't hurt," she said.

"What . . . what is that stuff?"

"You made it," said Judith. "Didn't you?"

Autumn recalled now marching back from having yelled at Rory Holt in the street and bursting in here, stumbling from cupboard to cupboard, only her anger keeping her going, her head in a fog. She'd made something completely instinctively, with her brain switched off, like when she'd made that potion at Christmas to save herself from a spell, but this time with nobody in the driver's seat but sheer emotion. "Yes," she said. "I made it. What does it do?"

Judith put a hand on her shoulder, and roughly turned her to look at the opposite wall. On it, the still steaming black goo had been painted into a rough circle. Autumn remembered now the physical action of making the shape with the brush.

"It's . . . the same shape as the one we saw in the pool," said Lizzie.

Judith went to the sink, turned on the tap, and put her hands under the water. Then she threw what seemed an unfeasible amount of it onto the floor. She took the bottle from the pocket of her cardigan and squirted whatever that was onto the surface again. Autumn thought distantly that she wouldn't like to risk doing the washing up in Judith's kitchen. Judith's idea of potion storage relied on her formidable memory and a make-do attitude that was like a magical version of *Blue Peter*. She banished the thought. Too happy. She couldn't allow herself that comfort either. She was going to have to face what she'd done here. And she had a terrible feeling she now knew what it was. "What . . . we saw earlier," she whispered. "Was that Old Rory's kitchen? Did I . . . was that his silhouette?"

"All light still exists, somewhere," said Judith, ignoring the question. "You just have to find it and get on the right end of it." An image of that kitchen formed, and Judith once more touched it with her toe. "There. Now let's rewind."

She spun the image anticlockwise and it dissolved into a rainbow. Judith seemed to judge how long she had to wait, then put her toe down again. In the pool, Autumn saw Rory Holt in what, yes, must be his own kitchen, walking about, maybe intending to make tea. He looked drunk and furious, slamming cupboard doors.

He turned at what must have been a sound and stumbled back, incredulous.

Into the picture stepped Autumn. She also looked drunk and furious.

"I'm sorry," said Autumn now.

"Be silent," whispered Judith, in a voice Autumn had never heard from her before. It had sounded utterly condemnatory, with the experience of centuries behind it.

"You must have used magic to get in," whispered Lizzie. Still keeping up that running commentary. As if it was the only help she could provide.

In the image, Autumn advanced on Rory, yelling at him, pointing at him. He started to yell and gesticulate back, to indicate he wanted her out of his house. He grabbed for a saucepan and brandished it like a weapon.

"You . . . thought he was going to attack you—" began Lizzie.

But Autumn in the image didn't look threatened. "Don't, Lizzie."

In the pool, Autumn turned on her heel, and triumphantly stepped back out of frame. Rory looked alarmed once more. He put down the pan.

He flew backwards.

He hit the wall. The black ash burst from where he hit, in his shape.

Autumn looked up from the pool and at the faces of her friends. "Did I . . . disintegrate him? Or did he go through the wall? No, they . . . would have found him if he went through—"

"You didn't kill," said Judith. "Though I'm glad you're feeling the weight of that. What you really did is summat that you might find harder to understand. Summat worse."

"How could it have been worse?"

"Watch." Judith used her foot to manipulate the image again, going back to the moment when Old Rory flew backwards. Then she spun the picture once more, to find . . . nobody there.

"So I'd gone?" said Autumn. "I mean, did I leave the moment after I . . . I blasted—?"

"Hold on." Judith held the view where it was and "rewound" as she had before. Autumn saw herself triumphantly step back through the hole in the wall, stick two fingers up at Rory, and vanish, the hole closing, leaving only the circle. Judith froze the image and spun it again, to show Rory in the act of putting down the pan.

And *then* he flew backwards.

Autumn felt sheer relief surging through her.

Until Judith stepped right up to her, furious. "Don't look relieved, you idiot!" she bellowed.

"Hey! I didn't hurt him!"

"Oh, didn't you? Look!" Judith threw something at her from out of her pocket. It was some sort of dust. Autumn flinched . . . and then realised nothing about her had changed, or . . . no, looking down, something seemed to now be wrapped all around her. Had that old witch . . . tied her up? No. No. She couldn't feel whatever this was, she could only see it.

She went to the full-length mirror in the corner and saw what it was. All around her were wrapped . . . they looked like fibres made of light, hundreds of them, in different colours. They led off from her in many directions, taut, attached to unseen anchors, fading where whatever Judith had thrown on her ended its influence. She was so wrapped up in them it was surprising she could move. She put a hand to them, and it went right through. She could move because they were still intangible to touch, as they had previously been to sight. Even to her own magically enhanced sight.

Judith marched up to her again, grabbed her by the shoulders, and wrenched her round to face her. "Last night you marched right through every line of force attached to the town's borders. You did what fairies do, walk to what's inside places, only you had no idea what you were doing. The gestures and words we use when we do magic are sometimes about *limiting* what our emotions want to do. The worst of us realise that emotions can connect straight to magic and let that go to their heads, don't try to regulate it, and that's what you did last night. You smashed through everything in your way, and now you've got the boundaries wrapped round you like a . . . bull in a knitting shop. The boundaries. They're . . . what was I saying? No, shut up, this is important." Autumn watched, bemused, as Judith stepped away and took a moment to lean on something.

"Judith, are you all right?" Lizzie asked.

Judith just shook her head. This silence, this effect on the old woman, was scaring Autumn more than the yelling had. But before she could start to argue, Judith had turned again and raised a finger to resume berating her. "Do you see? When you heaved off out of his kitchen, Old Rory was caught in the backlash and sent flying like he was on a catapult, off into who knows where. That's probably what's happened to the lorry driver that's gone missing. It might be what's happened to however many bloody people were at that dance or whatever it is that we're still hearing. And it's why the prince had so much trouble coming to see the reverend this morning. That's why I say what you did was worse than murder. You might or might not have hurt Rory. But you've hurt all the rest of us. Maybe everyone in the world. You've done what nobody's ever done, messed up the borders around Lychford. Now every dark thing that's out there, soon as they realise, they'll be heading here to mess with us. Some of the great nations too. There'll be summat happening among the fairies. And I don't know if there's anything we can do about it. All because you'd had a few!"

Autumn looked to Lizzie. She didn't look away, but was there something on her face of what Shaun had had in his expression earlier? "Well . . . what are we waiting for?" she shouted, her guilt bursting out of her as anger. "If it's so bloody urgent, shouldn't we be out there finding those people?" *And not in here accusing me of something I'm utterly guilty of.*

"Don't you take that tone with me. Don't you take any tone now." Judith was still blazingly angry. "I'm only waiting for—" There came a buzzing sound from the pocket of her dress. She put her hand in and pulled out a kitchen timer. "—right. My defences are ready. Come on."

And with that Judith headed for the door, and Autumn was horrified to see that she was actually running.

# 2

Lizzie would normally, for the sake of her exercise tracker, have been grateful for the opportunity of an impromptu jog, but when it was across the town, following a pensioner who was now displaying an astonishing turn of speed, with the future of everything at stake, well, that wasn't really one of the workout settings. Judith was sprinting, and sustaining it. There were cheers and laughs as they dashed past the locals. That could not, Lizzie was sure, be done without supernatural help. It must have taken some restraint, in her younger years, for Judith not to have tried out for the Olympics.

But restraint was what Judith was all about, wasn't it? And the lack of it was the great sin she was judging Autumn for. But was there something else, alongside that? Lizzie had a good ear for the interactions between people experiencing trauma, and beneath Judith's fury at Autumn, there seemed to be some unspoken anger, something personal. How gently, she wondered, had Autumn been dealing with her employee's grief? Or had she heard only stubbornness and replied in kind? And what about in the other direction? Autumn had been down and put upon for months, and Lizzie really hadn't been paying enough attention to that.

This was what their lives were now, that Lizzie not being there for her friends often enough might have led to the end of the world.

Surprisingly, since she had mentioned her defences being cooked, Judith led them not to her house, but up the hill to the Tatchell farm, baked mud flying from her sensible shoes. The sun was now beaming down on the three figures as they rushed up the spine of the bare hillside, along the track beside Tatchell's field of ripening wheat.

Judith staggered to a stop, stretched out her arms, and spun slowly, as if seeking something. Autumn just about fell beside her, until Lizzie grabbed her and managed to get her to her feet. But then Autumn started to throw up. Only another intervention by Lizzie stopped it from going over Judith's ankles.

"Over here," said Judith, not bothering to notice. She pointed and marched off across the corn, not caring about damaging the crop.

"Are you okay?" Lizzie asked Autumn, helping her to follow. At least the visible threads that had been wrapped around her had faded in the last few minutes. That dust, presumably, was wearing off.

"Of course I'm not bloody—! Sorry. What she was saying, about what I'd done, how . . . I guess, bad magicians? How they use this stuff? Am I going to 'the dark side'?" Lizzie could hear the irony she'd put into the words. "Like I'm becoming the stuff we're keeping out. Which is . . . what they've been saying to me, or not ever saying out loud. What they've been thinking."

Lizzie didn't like the sound in her friend's voice. "You've been under a lot of pressure, and I haven't been listening enough."

"I want to confess."

"Well, we don't do that very much in the C of E, but absolutely, you can confess to me and I can—"

"I don't want to be absolved. I want to take responsibility for this. Do you think there's some sort of . . . magical court, maybe with the fairies?"

"Shut up!" called Judith from ahead. "Move faster." They came to a grassy patch in the middle of the field, which stood out in the middle of the crop. Now they'd stopped running, Lizzie could still hear the distant dance music. Judith squatted slowly down and picked up two spades, which Lizzie was pretty sure hadn't been there a second before. "Dig," she said, "quick."

Autumn grabbed a spade, and set about digging. She was trying to demonstrate her commitment. "Those threads you saw wrapped around me," she said, "won't me moving about keep on disturbing them?"

Judith made a tutting noise, like this question was an unwanted burden. "The web of them is loose now. Dun't matter what you do."

Lizzie saw pain pass across Judith's face once more. "Are you okay? Doing all this, running like that, you have to pay a price, don't you? That's how it works."

Judith gave her a look that said further questions along those lines would be most unwise.

Lizzie sighed and started to dig. "How is there a grassy patch here?" She wasn't going to let Judith or Autumn lapse into brooding.

"Paul the builder is one of that lot that goes out with metal detectors. He thinks he found summat huge out here a few months back. He's got an agreement with Joe Tatchell to not sow on this bit, and he'll poke around after harvest."

"And what's that got to do with what we're doing?"

"He found an illusion I'd planted at this spot so he'd do all that. In case we ever had to do this. I'm up for fighting the powers of evil, but I'm not so stupid as I'd take on a farmer."

"But what happens when he realises it's not here?"

"I know what that lot with the detectors are like. He'd have kept poking around for it, year after year. So the spot'd stay put. Right. That's deep enough." She took from her cardigan pocket a tiny cloth bag with thread knotted at the top. "I kept these in the freezer. I had to put them in the oven when I realised what she'd done."

She'd addressed that explanation only to her, Lizzie realised. It was as if Autumn had become useful only for digging. Autumn had realised that too, and was looking helpless. "And they got into your pocket how?" asked Lizzie.

Judith gave her another look. "What do they call him, the green chap?"

"Is that someone we know, or—?"

"On schoolbags. He were on television when I were younger." It took a bit of interrogation before Lizzie realised Judith was talking about The Incredible Hulk. "Right. Him. If I go like him, knock me around the head with the brown-handled spade. That should fix it." And before either of them could ask any alarmed questions, even about why it had to be that particular spade, she'd put the cloth of the bag to her lips and started to blow into it.

Lizzie and Autumn looked at each other. "You've got the brown-handled spade," said Lizzie.

Autumn quickly swapped spades with her.

Judith's face was changing colour, but it was turning bright red rather than green. She seemed to have been blowing for an impossibly long time, drawing air from who knew where. Lizzie took a covert look behind the old woman and saw that her floral dress had flattened against the back of her legs, as if being pulled in by . . . no, she really didn't want to think about that.

Judith finally stopped, staggered, righted herself, and, with a little cry of pain, threw the bag into the hole. Light burst from where it struck the soil, and a pillar of it shot up into the sky, a light only they could see. Then it began to slowly fan out, dissipating into a vague glow that followed an arc.

"Basic defence," panted Judith. "Until . . . if . . . we can knit the boundaries back into place . . . it'll have to do."

"So now do we go after the lost people?" asked Autumn.

"In a bit." Judith looked like she didn't like speaking directly to Autumn now. She also looked on her last legs, her face grey with effort. "We've got three more of these to do first."

---

They raced around Lychford in the heat, putting the cloth bags into prepared sites that were, in order: inside the bole of a tree; by the side of a road, which needed a paving stone to be heaved up and got them curious shouts from drivers; in the playground underneath the slide, which required more digging. All the while, the distant beat of the dance music continued.

"Does it have to be here?" said Lizzie, about digging under the slide, aware that if anyone saw her she'd have some serious explaining, or rather lying, to do to the town council. At least she was getting her steps in today.

"I'm not responsible for where the cardinal points are. I just did my best to get these within twenty feet." Judith had done the same trick with the bags at three sites now, and now she embarked on it one last time. Lizzie seriously wondered if it would kill her.

Finally, she dropped the last bag into the hole and they filled it in. The light this time flashed up, connected with the other beacons, and from this angle they could now see they were inside a barely perceptible dome, which faded. But Lizzie could still feel the slight sense of added safety its continuing presence imparted.

Judith sat down on the grass. "Right," she said. "Now we can . . . can find those . . ."

"Let us do it," said Autumn.

Judith was silent for a long moment, her eyes closed. Lizzie hoped she'd say something comforting, but when she finally spoke, it was as bitter as before. "You've done enough."

"Do we know if anything's got through?"

Judith opened her eyes and started to push herself up.

"It will have. Maybe a few things, at random, shunted here like Rory Holt and the lorry driver and the rave were shunted elsewhere, or maybe loads of 'em, deliberately, if they were waiting ready to seize their chance."

"Refugees coming over the border," said Autumn. And now her voice was as hard as Judith's had been.

Judith finally looked at her. "It's not a bloody metaphor," she said. "Everything isn't about you."

She'd hauled herself to her feet and set off before Autumn could find a reply. Lizzie put a hand on Autumn's arm. The look on her face was a battle between anger and absolute guilt. "Just let me try to fix it," Autumn whispered. "Please. She has to let me try."

———

As the three of them marched down the river toward the route to the woods, Autumn kept looking at Judith. She kept waiting for the old woman to say that Autumn was no longer her apprentice, that after the lack of care she'd shown, she wasn't worthy. Autumn would have welcomed that. She would have got angry at it too, she couldn't help but react like that, but . . . oh God, when was Judith going to say it?

What would Lizzie be thinking now, if she'd been the one who'd done this? Would she be seeking judgment?

Would her guilt be so extreme? How much had the town Autumn had grown up in made the feeling seep into her skin that, being the only black person here, anything abnormal might be her fault? But no. The thought that she'd allowed this to happen because of how this place had treated her . . . that was a luxury she couldn't allow herself. Not if she wanted to retain her mental health. That was what other people liked to think of people like her. She wanted to take responsibility. She would find a way.

And yet, that whole circle of awful thoughts was something that would never even have occurred to Lizzie.

They entered the woods, and after a while came to the signpost that marked the point where some routes seen only by those such as them headed off in directions that could never be recorded on any map. It felt . . . different now. Judith sniffed the air. "Borders have moved here too," she said. "Right, so, we have at least one thing that's continuously leaking across the boundaries."

"What?" asked Lizzie.

"That bloody music." And yeah, there it was, still. "So that's the first thing we can work with. Try to figure out where it's coming from."

The three of them looked around, and managed, between them, to triangulate a direction for the varying beats. They set off that way, through the woods. "Time might be different where they are," said Autumn, remembering her own experience of journeying to fairy. "They'd have shut down the music and gone home by now otherwise."

No reply from Judith. It was as if she hadn't spoken.

After a while, they came to a halt as they all realised, just about at the same time, that the direction the sound was coming from had suddenly shifted, moved to somewhere behind them.

"It's like in a video game," said Lizzie, "when you're right on top of the marker you're trying to find, and it kind of slides away around you."

"I dunno what that means," said Judith, "but now I see what's gone on. The . . . rave, is it? It's caught in what we call a knot, a little loop of border stuff that she made when she went crashing through them."

"I think you should start using Autumn's name again," said Lizzie.

Judith ignored her. "There'll be different knots all over the place. The ends knit when they're thrown together, so they form little bubble worlds. I saw it once before, when I were younger. In . . ." She paused for a long moment, and a frown crossed her face. "Don't remember. Don't matter. Where was I? Oh ah. The rave might be in one, the lorry driver in another, Rory Holt in another."

"Do we know how many of them there are?" asked Lizzie.

"Dunno. Could be half a dozen, could be thousands. What worries me most is, are those people alone in there? These aren't just bits cut off from this world. She made the borders fly about, get mixed up and connected to each other, so there'll be bits of the other worlds in there too. There might be stuff that's got into the wrong places, dark things we've been trying to keep out, but have fallen into the knots."

"I think we really should try to find another word for 'evil' other than—" began Lizzie, who'd obviously seen the look on Autumn's face.

"Words I use aren't what's wrong. What she did is what's wrong."

Autumn took a deep breath and shoved it all down inside her once again. "Okay. How do we get into these knots?"

Finally, Judith addressed her. Because she knew what she was about to say was arrogant and annoying. "You can't get there from here."

"Then how—?"

"Not by walking, not by knowing stuff. We need to be lost. Close your eyes, put your fingers in your ears, and start walking."

"What about our, you know, other senses? The ones we got from the well?" asked Lizzie.

"They'll be what get us there. But not if we let our normal senses get in the way. This is like . . . looking for sum-mat really small. Summat that's curled up inside summat else. We need to concentrate. And not. At the same time."

Autumn did her best to follow those ridiculous in-structions. At last she could do something. She put her fingers in her ears, closed her eyes, and took a hesitant step forward, muttering "one potato, two potato . . ." to drown out any external noise. She let her feet lead her, moving slowly, expecting every moment to walk into a tree. She didn't know where Lizzie and Judith were. She realised, after a minute or so, that it was actually quite amazing that she *hadn't* walked into a tree. The air around her seemed to have suddenly got colder.

When she reached one hundred potatoes, she decided now would be a reasonable time to stop. She opened her eyes and took her fingers out of her ears.

It was suddenly night.

She was still in the woods, but now all was illuminated by a full moon. Yeah, it had been a full moon last night. And it was a summer night, but it was still bloody freez-ing compared to the brilliant day she'd been in a moment ago, and she was only wearing a dress.

She looked round for Judith and Lizzie, who she'd as-sumed would be somewhere behind her, but . . . no. She took a couple of steps, called their names, and realised she would have seen them by now.

She was . . . alone here.

And she didn't know how to get back. Because Judith hadn't told her that part. Perhaps it would be just about retracing her steps? Yeah, okay, let's go with that for now. So, she had to find if anyone else was in here with her. And hope like crazy that nothing . . . she refused to think of it as "dark" . . . that nothing with evil intent was in here too.

She hugged herself. So she'd successfully entered an area that still looked like it was part of the woods, but where it was still the night before. Because, right, time must be running more slowly in here. So this was . . . probably . . . hopefully . . . a knot that had got snipped off of their own world, and was somehow stuck in this previous time. How was she moving and breathing, then? Nope, can't answer that yet.

She realised she now couldn't hear the dance music at all. All was silence. So the illegal rave wasn't in here. Tick that off the list.

What if Rory Holt was here? How would he react if he saw her? That would be an interesting conversation. Please let him be alive for that.

Cautiously, she started moving through the woods, listening, alert for any sign of movement. But all was still under that big moon. At least moving kept her a bit warmer. The sweat from all that running about was swiftly cooling off.

After a few minutes, she saw something strange ahead of her. Along the top of a ridge, a number of the trees had fallen, a great fan shape of them, with soil tumbling from their exposed roots, turning the climb ahead into a slippery slope. It was as if something had knocked them over. She heaved herself up, stepped carefully over the timber, crested the ridge, and saw that, somewhere in the hollow below, obscured by fallen trees, a cluster of artificial lights was shining. "Hello?" she called.

She thought she heard a sound in reply. Perhaps a call for help. Cautiously, Autumn began to pick her way down the slope.

———————

Lizzie took her hands away from her face and looked round, startled at the sudden proximity of the dance music. Judith was standing at her shoulder. The sky was light with approaching dawn, the full moon of last night on the horizon. So, right, they'd gone back in time . . . or something. Ahead of them, flashing lights shone through the trees, the music blaring from that direction. She looked quickly around and then turned back to Judith. "Where's Autumn?"

Judith looked, if anything, more shocked than Lizzie felt. "She . . . she must have walked far enough ahead to stumble into . . . another knot."

"Right," said Lizzie. "Okay. Can we get her back?"

Judith shook her head. "When we unpick this, iron out the boundaries, we'll find her then, maybe . . ."

Why was the old witch suddenly looking so uncertain? "So if we just went back the way we came, then walked as far as she did—?"

"You don't just go backwards to get out. It's a whole other thing."

"What other thing?"

Judith's face was now a complete blank. Lizzie wondered for a moment if she'd stopped recognising her. Was this the toll for what she'd done today? If so, it had come at entirely the wrong moment. "Complicated," Judith said, finally.

Lizzie was damn sure she wasn't going to take more than a step away from Judith before she explained. She wanted to say if Judith hadn't been too angry to talk directly to Autumn she might have done the responsible thing and told both her apprentices how to get out of what she was leading them into. "Couldn't you have stopped her?"

"Not my fault if she walked off that quick."

"You do get that she's trying to prove herself?"

"Dun't matter. I can't train someone that goes and does this."

"When you were her age, you messed up so badly you ended up being cursed!"

Judith glowered at her. "I don't have to keep you on, either."

Lizzie was suddenly very calm. Which was what tended to happen when she got to the end of her tether. "Right now, especially, you need someone telling you the truth. You *hate* that you just let your apprentice walk into danger. I know you do. You're on your last legs. There's clearly stuff you're not telling me. You need our help. And you and she really need to sit down and talk about all of this—!"

"Don't you lecture me!" Lizzie was taken aback. She'd never heard Judith bellow like that before. The old woman took a few steps back, her fingers flexing, as if making a great effort to control herself. "I have never, ever, in my life, been spoken to like—"

And then she vanished, like she'd suddenly fallen backward through an invisible wall.

Oh no. Oh no. Lizzie swore out loud several times. "Judith?!" She stepped quickly forward, muttering a prayer, eyes closed and fingers in her ears . . . and stopped when she hit a tree. She was still in the same space. She'd walked right over the spot where Judith had vanished.

She tried a few more times, but it wasn't working. Maybe it was just that the sound of the rave was too great to ever be entirely blocked out of her ears.

She had no choice but to give up. She turned and headed toward the rave. She had no idea what she could do to get these people out of here, but at least if something nasty was in here with them, then . . . okay, she'd cross that bridge when she came to it. Damn it.

———————

Judith spun round, and yelled in anger. Then she turned again, reflexively. Gone! The reverend was gone too! No . . . actually, it was Judith herself who'd gone.

Stupid old woman. Where had she—?

Wherever it was, it was extraordinary.

There was nothing about this place that was like a place. It was like . . . a bunch of echoes, of sound and of light, rebounding endlessly, arcing all round her. She could breathe, but she felt it when she breathed in, it was something that was only trying to be air at the moment it hit her nose and mouth. There was nothing deceptive about that, it was a desperate attempt to welcome her, to keep her alive. But it didn't feel like there was thought behind it, either. It felt like . . . a fairground ride, summat automatic, summat that was creaking, that was being pushed too far.

She took a step, and the light and sound changed

around her again. The thick air slid past her hands, maybe only skin deep. Fire, the place said, fire was near, only the world was shielding her from it, keeping her alive when she shouldn't be here.

She closed her eyes, trying hard not to panic.

She was so tired. It felt like she was going to faint, and if she did, she didn't quite know how she was going to wake up again. She'd been using it up today, burning it up so fast . . . No. She made herself shake her head and found that place inside her where she would always be tough with herself. *Come on, girl. Hold on. Those two need you to get out of here and find them. Not that they deserve . . . no, enough of that. Enough. Now. Where have you got to?* It didn't seem like she was in the worst of the many possible situations she could have ended up in. There were worlds which had informed . . . and she'd had conversations with a couple of Lizzie's predecessors about this . . . the human idea of hell. It wasn't that they were all pitchforks and fire. It was that they were *about* the person who'd stumbled into them. Those worlds responded to people's fears, or even to their desires. If this was one of them, well . . . that would make her life into a fine shaggy dog story, eh?

But no. She was pretty sure this world was genuinely trying, with all its strength, to help her. The problem was that it didn't have much strength left.

She opened her eyes again, and made her mind seek . . . land, a horizon, summit to get a fix on. And then, slowly, there were shapes, she was making herself adjust, and the land was helping her, showing her ways to see. The light rolled around her and showed her how far everything was in every direction.

Oh. It was a bubble. A literal bubble. A piece of space from another world, then, where time continued as normal, but which had been sealed off from its surroundings. This would actually be the easiest sort of knot to explore, to find anyone in. Of course, if there were a nasty in here, it would also be easy for it to find her.

How had she come here while absolutely not blocking out all the noises and sights of a world that had had a rave in it?

Oh. It had been anger, damn it. For the first time in decades, she'd let the pure force of magic run through her, uncontrolled, as she'd been thinking about how to traverse the knots. She'd only gone and bloody well done exactly what Autumn had done. This individual knot, still taut, had burst open to let her in. At least no more harm could be done.

She took a few steps forward, and then, sure she was now calm and aware enough to not fall into any knots within knots, she began to walk more confidently. She wished she had brought her stick. The physical energy she had mortgaged against her future well-being was slowly leaving her.

A flat surface, black like obsidian, but not reflecting, had appeared ahead of her and under her feet. She'd made it come to her. This place knew it needed help. In the "sky" above, the light was still whirling and rebounding. So little space for it to play in.

Ahead, on the surface, she saw something.

A set of footprints was materialising. There was someone else in here.

Judith gave a little groan and made to follow.

---

Autumn had stumbled down into the hollow, and had immediately realised what the lights were. At the end of a trail of destruction, where it had carved a road for itself across the wooded hill, a huge articulated lorry lay on its side. She'd run to the cab, managed to put a foot on one of the wheels, and had climbed up onto the side of it. She'd looked inside, and tried the door. When it had clicked open, she'd managed to haul it upwards and look down into the interior.

There sat a battered man, in his thirties, stubbled chin, donkey jacket, cropped hair. He had a kind, frightened, bemused face. He was out of his seat belt, having managed to heave himself into an upright position. He looked up at her in relief. "Thank you. Where? What happened?"

Was that a Polish accent? Autumn decided she couldn't answer his questions very well in any language. And even then, the undercutting voice in her head added, she'd have hesitated to get to the point where his plight was her fault. "Are you hurt?"

"My leg, maybe broken. Hurts like . . . hell."

Autumn was moved that he'd felt the need to spare her delicate sensibilities from a swear word even in a situation like this. She swore in reply, and he managed a smile. In the movies, lorries in these circumstances would always explode, but she was pretty sure that didn't really happen, and there was no petrol smell, and if he'd been here an hour already it would probably have happened by now. If they'd been back in Lychford, she was pretty sure the best thing would have been to leave him where he was and keep him company until the emergency services got here. Pity she didn't have that option. "Have you seen anyone else?"

"I thought . . . someone moving. About ten minutes. I have been shouting."

Autumn raised her head out of the cab and looked carefully around. Everything was silent, apart from the wind moving the trees. The wind and the moon . . . she realised that this pocket she'd created couldn't be cut off in space, or the area cut off must stretch to the moon, and she was pretty sure it would have been missed. So that must mean it was . . . cut off in time? Or something? The moon didn't seem to have moved since she'd got here. What would walking through this place be like for someone outside the knot, who hadn't carefully got lost to find it? Would those unaware hikers suddenly hop to a moment later, a moment that was missing from the world? Would they even notice?

These were the sort of questions Judith never liked her asking. Mainly because the old . . . witch didn't know the answers. Magic let you jump over the "why" and make use of what was hidden, all from the comfort of your kitchen sink.

She didn't think she'd ever stop needing to know why. Maybe that, too, didn't make her a very good apprentice. Just as well she wasn't going to be one for much longer. That thought gave her an ache she knew she deserved. She dismissed it.

She ducked back down into the cab. "Does your radio work?"

It took a bit of miming and explaining to translate the word "radio," but when he got it, he switched it on, and Autumn listened to a single sustained note of early hours music on Radio 1. It took her a few moments to realise it wasn't the more experimental end of the dance spectrum, but that it was going to go on like that forever. She switched it off again.

She looked back out of the cab. She couldn't put this off any longer. That "first aid for small businesses" course she'd taken was finally going to pay off.

"Okay," she said, "it's going to hurt, but we have to get you out and mobile."

———

It had turned out the rave was in an abandoned building that looked like it had once been a cattle barn, a building that Lizzie had walked around a couple of times in the last few weeks when she'd been trying to get her steps in. A large generator on wheels was chugging away outside, and a crowd of young people were milling around, while more had been visible through the barn entrances, still dancing. Lizzie had heard a DJ shouting encouragement. It had seemed like the party was still in full swing.

Most of the crowd outside had been smoking or snogging or sobbing, doing what the people outside clubs always did, but a few of them had seemed to be talking urgently, looking worried. Those were the ones who'd looked up, surprised, as Lizzie had approached. As if they'd been hoping someone would arrive.

One of them, a young man with a big grin and a bigger beard, had stumbled over to her, his arms outstretched. His friends had followed. "It's a vicar!" he'd cried, and, to Lizzie's surprise, he'd moved in for a surprisingly sincere hug. Sincere, but, err, he'd obviously been dancing all night. There was a certain moistness. She'd gently disengaged herself. "I'm not religious," he'd assured her, loudly and immediately, "but I love that you are, like these woods are, like those birds are. Those starlings. They're religious."

Lizzie had never previously encountered someone who, prior to asking her name, had ventured theories concerning ornithological theology. "I suspect," she'd shouted over the music, "that you may have been on more than the cider."

"Oh no! You got me! Will I go to hell?"

"I tell you what," Lizzie had said, "you tell me about a few things, and then take me to whoever's in charge, and I'll do my best to make sure we avoid that."

Which was how she was taken into the presence of a man who she was told was "Stewie, just Stewie," who'd been standing at a little distance from the barn, toying with his phone.

He laughed when he saw her. "Here we go! Is this a delegation from the town?"

Lizzie didn't want to get into whos and whys. "How

long do you feel you've been up here?"

"Look, we'll be off as soon as it's dawn. This isn't up for discussion. If I see you reading number plates or taking photos, churches have stained glass windows, right? What's that they say about people in glass houses keeping their noses out of my business?"

The bearded lad who'd brought her over stepped in, his hands raised. "Hey. Hey. No need for that."

Stewie just smiled as one would at the actions of a toddler.

Lizzie found herself just a little bit pleased that she knew more about this situation than Stewie did. "What if dawn never comes?"

"Is this, like, a metaphor you're going to use in your sermon?"

"No, listen, Stewie, something's going on up here." The lad was insistent. "That's what we've been trying to tell someone. We can't get to the cars."

Stewie was about to go back to playing with his phone, but Lizzie put a hand on his arm, and he looked pleasingly startled at the force of her grip. "How about you show us where the cars are, and then I promise I'll wander off home to my quaint little church?"

———————

Judith had been following the footprints that were being shown to her. She could feel the morning's exertions sapping her strength every moment, but would she notice it getting to her noggin as well? She was better in the afternoons than the mornings. After lunch was when she tended to write angry notes to herself and attach them to the fridge.

She'd lost so much strength today, so much that she'd never get back.

If she bloody lost track of what was real ... *No, don't think about that now, you stupid old woman, find who made these prints.* They were made by a bloke's shoes, by the look, but you couldn't be sure of that these days.

She turned at a sound. And realised she had company. Floating in the light above her were five extensions of that light, like weird, shifting interruptions of her vision. Arcs of light flew between them, blazing and extinguishing in a moment. Maybe this was the place migraines came from.

Judith knew that the real world of magic wasn't like Harry Potter. Everyone had different names for the beings that came from the other worlds that bordered on theirs. And the degree to which those things recognised and understood human beings depended on how much they'd interacted with human cultures. The fairies, for instance, had a long tradition of cultural exchange. Which usually went one way, mind you, but at least their lust and avarice and anger meant they took the time to magic up human languages.

This lot . . . well, she had so little to go on. "Good morning," she said. Which was more polite than she'd be to most human beings.

They moved closer, interested, worried, maybe aggressive.

"Do you like mints?" She reached into the pocket of her cardigan and brought out a rather old packet of black and white striped ones. "They're very bad for me."

A jolt of light hit the packet, grabbed it, and threw it aside.

Judith was about to start telling the damn thing off, because it was either that or lose control of her bowels when there came, from behind her, something that was a mixture of a bellow and a scream.

A figure leapt out of nothingness, grabbed her, and hauled her away in a moment to an area of the black surface where the beings were no longer present. She was pretty sure, mind you, that in a space this small, they hadn't actually lost track of her, but had held back from following.

The man, because it was a man, looked around urgently. He was shaking with fear. But now Judith had realised who it was. "Rory Holt," she said.

"Judith Mawson? Oh, that's right, you work for her, don't you? Did she get you too?"

Judith didn't know quite how to answer that.

"We should be safe this far into the bush," he continued. "She teleported us to another planet, like on *Star Wars.*"

Judith realised that his senses, limited, unlike hers, to what he'd been born with, were making an entirely different sort of sense of what was around them. "If that works for you," she said.

"What the hell did you think you were doing, offering those monsters sweets? I hid as soon as I saw 'em. You reckon she'll come back to finish us off? All right, we can't talk here, come back to my camp and you tell me everything you know."

And he grabbed her hand and hauled her off. He couldn't perceive how small the world he was in was, Judith quickly realised. They were actually walking like two idiots in some theatre show, pretending to go for miles with big, silly steps as the ground rolled beneath them.

———

With much yelling on his part, Autumn had managed to get the lorry driver, whose name she'd learned was Marcin, out of his cab. She'd taken his weight and basically let him fall on her to get to the ground. He lay there, sobbing with pain, as she got to her feet and looked around again.

Still the silence. Still nothing moving. Still the feeling there was something out there.

She'd already found a suitable stick, and taken a roll of strong tape out of the back of the lorry. She knelt beside Marcin, and started wrapping the stick to his leg. As she worked, she tried to stay aware of her surroundings. But as she was pulling tight the last piece of tape . . . what was—?

Something was standing right beside her.

She leapt up, spun round. But there was nothing there. It had been just in the corner of her eye. But she was sure something had been there.

"Did you see anything?" she asked Marcin. It was obvious he hadn't.

She shook her head, checked the binding, and carefully helped him to his feet. The splint held.

"Good," he said. "Who are you? What do you, about—?" He indicated what was around them.

Autumn decided she had to tell him something. "Good witch," she said, pointing at herself. Not that she believed that in any sense of the words.

To his credit, Marcin only boggled for a moment. He put a finger to his nose and wiggled it. "Dee dee, dee dee . . ."

Autumn was glad she'd seen clips from *Bewitched* on-line. She joined in with humming the theme tune for a moment. "Yeah, and her spells kept going wrong too, with hilarious results."

"Witch with doctor, leg?"

She felt awkward. Not so much. "I try to do science too."

"Get us home, okay?"

"Okay—" And there was the thing in the corner of her eye again. This time she managed to stop herself from jumping, and tried to look sidelong at it. This was something that could keep itself just about hidden, even from her extra senses. It was just a white blur, a furtive figure, the same shape as a human being, but . . . no, she couldn't see any features.

She leapt back, sure that in that second it had moved to touch her. It had been the jerk of a predator striking. She felt like it had only just missed.

She grabbed the startled Marcin and heaved him up. "Come on!" she bellowed.

She was sure he could just about hobble along. But where could they run to?

———————

Stewie had sighingly headed with Lizzie and the bearded

lad to the makeshift car park. It should, it seemed, have been at the end of the lane that ran up the other side of the hill. But as they'd made their way through the trees, Stewie had got increasingly confused, had even stopped to look at the map app on his phone. Whatever he found had just made him swear. "How can we be lost? It was just over here."

Finally, having walked in a straight line, they'd returned to the barn.

"No," he'd said, turning slowly round. "No. Who put something in my water? You think that's funny?" He'd swung to point at Lizzie, his hand going to his back pocket, where he may or may not have had a knife. "Who are you?"

Lizzie had seen two large individuals in high vis jackets coming over to see what was agitating their boss, and had decided to put her cards on the table. "I'm your only chance of getting home."

It had taken some doing, but in the end, once the big lads had also gone to find the cars and returned from the wrong direction, startled looks on their faces, Lizzie had got Stewie to listen. He'd gone to the tent, got the DJ to switch everything off, and had shepherded the crowd, who were now sure the police were arriving, into an audience around them.

Lizzie had told them the truth, or as much as they

needed to know, and had found them, perhaps unsurprisingly, pretty easy to convince of just about anything. Not that what she was telling them hadn't created its share of sobbing, shouting, and hysterical laughter. At least while she'd been talking she'd come up with the start of a plan to get them out of here.

She pointed back to the tent. "We need to get that PA started up again."

They showed her how they did that, and she got up behind the DJ's mixing decks, on stacks of crates at one end of the barn. Thank goodness nobody was taking a photo of her. She would look like the worst possible trendy vicar. The DJ, who looked like she was about twelve, couldn't stop staring. "Could you turn up the volume to full?" Lizzie asked. She bent to the microphone. "Testing," she said. "This is Lizzie, calling Finn. Come in, Finn. Or anyone in the Court of the Unseen. Come in."

"It's not a radio," said the DJ, obviously wondering if the newbie knew anything at all about the world.

"But," said Lizzie, "I know the people I'm talking to can hear it."

———

Judith, getting tired of being dragged along like she was in a half-arsed mime troupe, had finally shouted to Rory

Holt to stop. She'd been about to tell him that she was here to rescue him, but then, over his shoulder, Judith had seen something appear out of the nothingness. She'd grabbed Rory, put a hand over his mouth, and, while he was wetly yelling into her palm, spun him round to see.

A group of the flying beings had gathered. More of them this time. Too many to count easily as they shifted and melted into each other. Between them was . . . this was their version of a device, she realised. It was a solid golden sphere that shot between them.

Rory stiffened in horror. "They've brought their cooking pot. That's meant for us."

Judith didn't believe for a second that that was what was going on here. "What do you see of what they're doing?"

"It's some kind of native religion. We're in Ooga Booga Land here."

Judith wondered what sort of books Rory had read when he was growing up. If they could see these beings now, it was because they wanted to be seen, though Rory was now miming parting foliage with his hands, as if he was spying on them at the edge of a clearing. "I think," she said, "these might be what some call sprites. There are loads of different ones. They're summat to do with elements, not like iron and whatnot, more like principles. This lot are fire sprites. Back when we lived in caves, they're meant to have come over and started campfires. To be on speaking terms with one was summat people boasted about, or more often kept to themselves. Then we get electricity and—"

"What are you going on about, woman?"

"—suddenly they're from 'Ooga Booga Land.'"

"But you can see them right there, see them with your own eyes."

"But we're seeing different things."

Rory was looking annoyed at her. "Here, I'm on your side, remember? You sound like her. She sent us here, so this is probably where she's from. She's been hiding among us, pretending not to be an alien, but now we know."

Judith didn't feel like arguing with this idiot. "Right," she said, and stepped forward to address the sprites. "Afternoon," she said, doing her best to put on her posh voice. For some stupid reason. "I think maybe we got off on the wrong foot." She looked over her shoulder and saw Rory hadn't followed her, but was still "hiding in the bushes," gesturing urgently for her to come back. "That one can't see you properly. But I bring the right tribute." She reached into the pocket of her cardigan and found her big box of household matches, the foundation of any good witch's pocket contents. She struck one, and solemnly held it up toward the sprites.

They seemed to confer for a moment, and just before even Judith with her Teflon fingers had to drop the match, the fire was sucked away to join their light. Judith looked between them. They'd taken care to position themselves to all get a bit of that flame. Judith took out match after match and lit them, letting them take the fire, until she only had a few left. She showed them those in the box. "Do you want to save some for later?"

From behind her, there came the noise of Rory slowly "stepping out of the bushes." "Wise woman make fire," he said. "Very powerful."

Judith sighed. If only he knew. "Can you understand me?" she asked them. The sprites paused for a moment. Then the golden ball flew at her and stopped an inch in front of her nose. On its surface was an image of a diminishing ball . . . or bubble. It got smaller even as Judith watched.

Judith swore under her breath.

"What is it?" said Rory. "Are they still thinking about eating us?"

Judith didn't know how to put it in terms he'd understand. This knot was collapsing. Very soon it would vanish out of existence. And they would almost certainly vanish with it.

# 3

Autumn had heaved Marcin along, putting all her hungover desperate strength into keeping him moving. Whatever was after them seemed to be like one of those predators in wildlife documentaries that circled their prey, then rushed in. Maybe her putting up a fight that time had made it wary. What did those documentaries say about facing a bear? Make yourself big and yell? Or was that for a mountain lion? Living in rural England, she hadn't paid much attention to those bits.

Marcin had been yelling questions at her, only about half of them in English. What were they running from? It hurt! He got to the point of actually fighting her off, and so, finally, she'd been forced to drop him. Now here they were, on a slight rise among some close trees, which Autumn hoped might give her some idea of when the thing approached. Marcin was lying on the ground screaming insults at her in Polish, and she was looking around, trying to watch out of the corner of her eyes. Which was really pretty bloody difficult. It kept making you want to just keep turning your head.

How the hell was she going to get him to close his eyes and put his fingers in his ears? Would the pain of his injury even let him lose concentration? Assuming that was actually how they could get out of this.

She needed to be able to see her enemy. What could let her see it better? What could let her see something the extra senses given to her by the well in the woods didn't let her see?

She realised. Today she had already experienced just that. That dust Judith had thrown over her. If she could find some . . . She looked desperately in her pockets, ran her hand through her hair. Thank God. Here was just a trace of it on her fingers. The dust that had actually worked must get used up as it did so. She had no idea what this stuff was, so she could only hope that Judith activated it just by thinking some magical power into it.

But, what could she actually do with it? She could throw this tiny handful of dust at whatever this thing was when she was sure it was near. That would give her something of it she could see. But having to let it again get that close . . .

Oh. Oh, she'd just thought of something awful.

No, she couldn't hesitate. If Judith had shown her anything, it was that magic was about sacrifice.

She held open her left eye with one hand, and with the other . . . she quickly rubbed the dust into the eye, thinking magical power into it as she did so. She could hear Marcin make an uncomprehending noise of fear.

The dust was very fine. It didn't hurt as much as she expected—

Her eye was suddenly on fire. She screamed.

She blinked and slowly the pain subsided, and the colours washed into half of her brain, and she had to close the other eye for a second, because now she could see . . . everything!

The knot they were in, she could see the lines of force all around it. It was really small, and it was . . . getting slightly smaller, all the time, she could *see* the tension in the coloured threads. She could see them moving. And oh God, they were, they were moving inwards!

She looked down and saw the threads that still wrapped round her, how they loosely led off to connect to . . . she could see the connections now. They ran off from her body in all directions, linked into a great weave that was wrapped around the knot, that was the knot, that also went beyond it. All she had to do was to concentrate on one particular aspect, the shrinking or the relative tension, or one colour, and there it was, at the front of her mind, clear to her sight.

She turned and looked at Marcin. He was swimming with colour, all the flavours and influences that had made him. She could see his family, their history, the big moments of his life, intimacies that she shied away from and regretted seeing, but . . . okay, overall feeling, here was a good guy, so thank all the gods she didn't believe in for that at least. She didn't know what the individual threads meant, she'd been seeing stuff at random, had no idea how to discern that part of it. That would be the next level of this deep structure, that lived underneath their own special senses, that Judith knew about and could access if she wanted to, but that she'd never bothered to . . . no, when had Judith not done what had to be done? It must be more like she'd never needed to examine it.

It was like Autumn had a tube map, but without any of the names of lines or stations.

Still, hell of a map.

She heard a sound behind her that she was pretty sure she couldn't have heard before, because the warning signal flared in her new sight too, a sudden burst of threads into her eye. She spun round.

And there was the creature. Right beside her. It had the shape of a man, but was almost a silhouette, a few lines of a sketch. Only it was stark white. It had no features, but Autumn knew it was looking at her.

Suddenly, it hopped from one side to the other, then back again. That was something that predators did, wasn't it? It was getting its eyes lined up on her, and it wasn't sure how strong she was.

Neither was she.

Slowly, keeping her eye on it, she reached down and helped Marcin to his feet. "You're . . . seeing a thing?"

"Yes, and it's real and it's right in front of us." She managed to get him upright, and was about to reach down to pick up the biggest nearby stick when she realised she was trying to get her hand past one of the coloured threads to do it, that she could feel them now, by touch as well, feel them wrapped around her like she was covered in a sort of . . . electric pullover.

This ability to see and feel the threads wouldn't last long. But it would last longer than they would if that thing attacked. However, it was planning to do that. She could pick up the stick or . . .

She didn't know what any of the threads meant or where any of them led. But now she could see how they fitted together. So if she just—

The creature leapt forward.

Autumn grabbed the nearest thread and heaved.

———

Lizzie had tried calling Finn's name into the microphone, and all the other names she'd heard associated with him. She'd waited, but no response had come. Of course, it was perfectly possible that he could hear her, but couldn't get inside the knot. Given how he'd walked into her house, however, despite the collapse of the borders into new shapes, she rather doubted that. The problem had previously been that he hadn't been able to find where this was.

So she'd started to describe their location, both geographically, talking about the old barn and the track that led up the hillside, and temporally, trying to precisely describe where the full moon was. Because, and a quick peep outside the barn had confirmed it, that moon was staying put.

Now she was elaborating on those details. The bemused DJ was looking on, convinced that she'd flipped. And yeah, maybe a lack of faith in her sanity right now would be appropriate. A shout came from outside. Then a whole bunch of yells and cheers and even screams.

Lizzie got up from the mike and ran for the door as the DJ did also.

Outside, the crowd were staring at . . . oh, there was a circle of day, bright summer day, blazing into the night of the woods like a searchlight. Lizzie squinted, blinked; she could just about see something in the light. Figures. Oh, and now the light was expanding, as if heaving against something. Great, this must be Finn; they were being rescued!

Suddenly the light burst through, and the night collapsed around them like a stage curtain, and they and the barn and the generator were all standing not in the woods, but in a bright, open summer meadow in broad daylight, with the most beautiful, invigorating fragrances blasting into their nostrils.

But Lizzie was now not so reassured. Because they weren't home. She knew this exaggerated version of her own world from distant sightings. This was the place Autumn had been left so scarred from visiting. This was a meadow in the land of fairy. And standing in it wasn't, as she'd hoped, a relieved and/or petulant Finn, but a trio of strange, thin beings who seemed to be reflecting the sunlight in mad, angular ways. She could just about perceive that they were wearing armour, an armour of green and gold, and had in their hands swords that were making the air around them sing with their sharpness, that were somehow breaking the very air that drifted across them.

She saw all of this with the new senses given to her by the well in the woods. She had no idea what the others were seeing, but whatever it was, it was making them huddle together and back away in alarm.

She took a look behind them. More of the same endless summer meadow, around a circle of mulch from the forest floor. The knot had collapsed, or been forcibly demolished, more like, and they'd been dropped into the middle of fairy.

The shouting from around her made her turn back. The three figures had stepped forward. Their shadows had suddenly lengthened and fallen over the cowering humans, deliberately, a show of force. Where the hell was Finn? He must work so hard, she thought, must have observed Autumn and the rest of them so closely to even pass as human. Because these fellows of his who weren't trying . . . they were something completely Other.

"You!" the lead figure bellowed, the word seeming to twist into a translated version as it got to Lizzie's ear. "This is our land now! You are inside! We want you out!"

---

Rory had been gesturing angrily at the sprites. "You send gods home, or gods get angry, gods strike you down, capeesh?"

Judith had wanted to ask what language, exactly, "capeesh" came from, but she'd suspected he didn't know. The sprites had been twisting in urgent conference. Rory had kept trying to get through to them on his own, limited, terms.

She'd been hoping the sprites might offer her some power she could use to get out of here. She'd been putting that off until she absolutely had to do it, because, though the spell she had to cast was clear in her head, she was terribly afraid of how much of her strength it would use. But no, these poor things could barely feed themselves, and no other solution was going to present itself, and she was feeling weaker rather than stronger, so . . .

What had she been thinking about? She put a hand to her brow.

Why had she been hoping the . . . whatever they were called . . . why had she been . . . ?

Oh God. Oh God. What were all these . . . things?! Where was she? Was she having a nightmare? Who was this old man? Where was her family? "Dad?!" she called out. Was this Dad? No, he didn't look anything like . . . but what did Dad look like? She should be able to re-member!

The old man was looking at her in horror.

---

Autumn had heaved her way through a glowing web of colour, rushing through it, grab and run, grab and run, one-handed, holding Marcin with the other, pushing all her rage and frustration into just getting past something she could finally connect with, something she could finally . . . rip through!

And then she was through it.

She stumbled out onto a . . . grey, empty expanse. She

looked around. It wasn't quite a world. Distant ... mountains? No, they faded again. They kind of shied away. It was like they were asking if she wanted to have mountains there, and when she'd mentally questioned that, they'd shyly retreated.

Marcin was gasping. She looked to him. He was looking round in horror. "Work," he said. "Work, all, nothing else, all life." She had no idea what his eyes were seeing. The expression on his face was that of someone who was in their own personal ...

Suddenly, walls sprang up around them. Bare walls with peeling paintwork, a smell of stale beer that made her once again want to vomit, a bar overflowing with ale pump signs for unreal brands all about bulldogs and Spitfires, and everywhere around her, Union flags and the cross of Saint George, and red, white, and blue bunting and suddenly hemming them in on every side, fat, white men in Union Jack waistcoats, wearing flat caps, laughing their heads off as they chinked their handled beer mugs together, the foam splashing over her in great waves. Their laughter urged her to join in, join in, join in.

She pulled Marcin, who was looking up and down at where to her there were gaps, seemingly in an entirely different world, to the door. She flung it open, but outside there was just more of the same. A television was on in here, and an ecstatic posh-voiced commentator was shouting, "It's us against the world now! The sun will never set on the land of hope and glory!"

Autumn slammed the door. She mustn't lose control. She had to think. That moment of mountains had been this place sizing her up, testing out her mind before finding out what sort of world she *didn't* want to be in and then flinging it at her. This was . . . oh God, this was actually hell, right? For anyone who came here. *A* hell, anyway. But how could there ever be anything more definitively hellish than torments that immediately suited themselves to you personally?

She looked back to the exact place they'd been when they entered, and now, to her shock, a new figure was squeezing its way through the laughing men, the thin white shadow that had pursued her earlier. It must have been so close behind them it had come here, too. It was cringing, its fingers clenching and unclenching, staggering, spinning around as if looking for release.

Oh God. It was suffering in its own private hell too. Whatever surrealism that involved, Autumn couldn't imagine.

She gathered all her courage, and heaved Marcin along to stumble toward it. Okay, it was time to make use of the rage she felt at everything that was crowding in around her here. She concentrated again on seeing the threads that underlay everything, while she still could, and sure enough, there they were, and seeing them made her stop in shock for a moment. Here they'd been twisted into a web that looked expertly woven, that wrapped round the heads of all three of them, that looked like they were the captives of some enormous . . .

She locked away that thought before this world realised how terrifying it was and made the fear real. She grabbed the threads and heaved.

And heaved . . . and heaved . . . and now she was simply pulling more and more of the stuff out of the air, building it up around her, wrapping it around her, trapping them more and more every second, and now it was billowing out of where she was pulling it, uncontrollably, and she realised that this place had latched on to that part of her fear too.

———

"Okay!" Lizzie had shouted to the leader of the fairies. "We're all for that! We want to get out and get back to our world as soon as possible!" Because, after all, this wasn't usually the problem with humans and fairies. The problem was usually that the fairies wanted the humans to stay. "But how do we do that?"

The fairies had been silent. Then they'd just taken another threatening step forward. And those shadows had once again lashed out with a sort of internal visual . . . roar.

"This isn't happening," Stewie had whispered beside her. "This is some . . . hallucination!"

"Then we're all having it," the bearded boy had whispered. He'd looked to her. "Who are they? What can we do?"

"They won't even tell us the rules!" the DJ had yelled.

Because, Lizzie had thought, there was something a bit stagey about all this. Was what happened here going to be related back to Finn's father, the king, as some sort of border incident, perhaps something Finn, as the go-between, should have prevented? The most worrying possibility was that if they were going to be portrayed as an invading horde, then their deaths might be a useful part of that portrayal. Not that the court were ever going to hear their version. Could this incident be used, even, to start a war? That was something the whole human race was unprepared for, never mind the three of them who supposedly guarded Lychford and now had not much in the way of boundaries to help with that.

She spoke up, aware that, following the lad's lead, more and more of these kids were looking to her. "We need to work out how to get out," she called to them. "How about we start by backing up to the edge of this?" She pointed to the ground where the circle of woodland soil and mulch around the barn, with trees still standing inside it, was a plain indicator of the area that had been in the knot, now not wrapped back around itself, but obvious against the shining green of fairy grassland.

They ran together, away from the fairies, to the edge of the circle. Lizzie quickly stepped across it. Nothing. There must be a way, a way which would be obvious, probably, from the fairies' own point of view, because otherwise how could they characterise this as an aggressive action?

She walked round the boundary, the others following her, hoping clearly that at any moment something magical would happen. Stewie was shaking his head, yelling that whoever had done this to him would pay, but the bouncers who'd come with her had serious looks on their faces. Those guys knew when they were in trouble.

Lizzie felt a vibration on her wrist. She looked at her exercise monitor. "Congratulations!" a tiny scrolling text read. "You've doubled your target!"

What? But she couldn't have gone further than . . .

She quickly stepped back over the same spot. Her wrist vibrated again. This time the device was ecstatic with the news that she'd trebled her target. If she did it again, the thing would probably give her the number of the nearest hospital. Whatever else happened to her today, she could die happy in the knowledge that she'd almost certainly beaten every other vicar in the weekly Diocesan Steps League. "Here," she said. "There's something wrong with space just here. I think this is the way out."

They all gathered round, eager and hopeful. But, given that she hadn't immediately vanished home, what could she do with that knowledge?

———————

Judith suddenly realised someone was talking to her, talking to her like she was a bloody idiot. It was Rory Holt. He was staring into her face. "My wife went like this. Couple of years before she passed on. I know there's no getting through to you, but I have to try. Now's not the time for you to be away with the fairies."

Judith bridled at the expression, grabbed his shoulder, and hauled herself to her feet. It wasn't his words that had brought her back; her brain chemistry had just happened to sway in the right direction. She fought down a tremendous surge of panic. How much smaller had the bubble become? Oh no. Now it was like standing in a greenhouse. The sprites were clustered near them; soon they'd all be crushed into each other. What was the spell she needed to recite to get them out? She was so stressed she still couldn't think how it started. She reached into the pocket of her cardigan for some more of that dust that would at least let her see the threads here, but she'd thrown it all at Autumn. "Stupid woman," she whispered. "I'm so stupid!"

"It's not your fault. It's that girl who sent us here." The sprites reacted with sudden light as the wall lurched in on them and Rory followed that with the nastiest words about Autumn that Judith could possibly imagine, all about her colour. "All her fault!" he spat again as the sprites rushed in fear around him. Heaven knew what he could see of them. Judith didn't want to know.

If it was the end now, Judith realised, she wanted to say summat true. Summat she'd only just started in this moment admitting to herself. "It's not her fault," she said, "it's mine. Mine a long time back. She made one mistake, I did exactly the same, and I was cursed for it, cursed for it so I suffered so long it took its toll on my noggin, and that's why you're stuck here, Rory Holt, because *I* made one mistake, and maybe you made a few too!"

The sprites cried out in light as the roof of the world fell in on them all.

---

Autumn had tried to think as the material that made the borders of the worlds ... what this place was *pretending* was that material in order to scare her . . . had flooded over her. But she'd quickly become lost under it, her world just chaos, nothing her flailing hands could grab hold of. No baseline to put her feet on, no rules.

But, she realised, that was what this place was trying to tell her, to scare her with, wasn't it? There were rules, she just had to dig deep and find them. For the sake not only of herself, but for helpless Marcin, who she could feel as if at a distance, shaking with his own fears. She even had to do it for the sake of that thing that had followed them. She had to do it for the sake of Luke, for everyone who . . . cared about her.

How could she get past the fear? What was her experience telling her to do?

Bloody bite it. Chew it. Rip it up.

She snatched at the material with her teeth, grabbed it and held on, wrenched it from side to side. Was this achieving anything? Only satisfaction, but . . . there was a taste here . . . what was that? Taste, like every other sense she had, had been changed by exposure to the water from the well in the woods, but it wasn't often she got to make use of it. There was a kind of . . . meaningfulness under the emptiness she had in her mouth, a sense that . . . yeah, put her tongue on it, get more of it . . . a sense that something real was here underneath.

Okay, what had she got to lose? She grabbed a handful

of what was turning into a void of meaninglessness around her and started to gulp it down. Started to take it like it was a drug. Come on, let her body and brain process this stuff, let it poison her, let her actually start to see what was . . .

She realised she'd started to see the real fibres again. That now they were leading right into her body, that she'd actually managed to randomly pull some of them into her. What if she went beyond being able to pull on them, actually got . . . ? She grabbed a great handful of them and shoved them into her mouth, and into her brain, and it pulled her open, and she pulled them open in turn, and she forced her way inside. She abandoned the idea of her brain making sense of what she was visualising, and went with the impossibility. She reached a hand out of the impossible knot that was impossible to get out of and grabbed Marcin and the white being and hauled them in after her.

Suddenly all three of them were in a sort of kaleidoscopic rollercoaster, colours rushing past at an impossible speed. Marcin was yelling, his hands trying to find purchase on something, but at least now he was reacting to the same thing she was. The being had just curled in a ball. But she herself . . . she was surfing this now. She had no control, but she could stand, and face forward, and see what was coming, ready to deal . . .

There was ahead a jumble of infinite threads, all colours, which she couldn't make sense of. The point where all the boundaries met, where all the borders were pulled tight. This was what someone had made, centuries ago, around Lychford. It connected the worlds as well as holding them apart. It wasn't a great work of art, it was an organic mess of compromises and solutions and traps.

Autumn fell into it yelling.

———————

"What the bloody hell," said Judith, "are you doing in my head?"

Judith hadn't actually expected to be alive. She was annoyed to find that she'd grabbed hold of Rory Holt as if to shield him from the collapse, just as he'd grabbed hold of whatever he could see of the sprites. They were all curled together in a tiny preserved bubble of a world, light flickering around them.

"Holding the roof up," said Autumn, from where Judith normally had an internal voice telling her to remember she'd put the kettle on or that *Gardeners' Question Time* would be on soon, "and hey, you're welcome."

"Just . . . don't look around, now you're in there!"

"I can't help it. I can . . . see . . . no, I'm feeling, I'm experiencing, like they're my memories too ... oh ... oh no, oh Judith, I'm so—"

Judith wouldn't have been able to stand her pity if they'd been in the same room, never mind when it was coming from between her own ears. "Get out!" she whispered.

"If I do that, there goes the roof. I didn't choose to be in here, I just landed in the centre of ... I think it's where all the boundaries are attached ... and I saw you here and I threw my ... my sort of hand ... out to save you and here's where I ended up."

"How the hell ... ? No, never mind that. Can you get us out of here?"

Judith felt Autumn's presence sort of ... shifting in her head, like she was now looking at summat else apart from every intimacy of Judith's life. The other thing Judith didn't like was ... oh, yes, she could feel Autumn's existence too. There was an outsiderness that Judith recognised, but that with Autumn was both of long standing and recently, sharply, deepened. Judith found they were suddenly thinking a thought in both their inner voices at once. It was that if she wanted to, Judith could move to another town and fit in, while Autumn would always have a certain number of people who stood between her and that release.

To share a thought ... when she was younger, that

would have been so good. But now it hurt so much. That outsider feeling was something Judith so did not want for Autumn, and she saw with great guilt how she had contributed to it. That guilt was reflected back by Autumn's thoughts about how she'd treated Judith, given how Judith . . . *was* now.

Oh. Oh no. What could be worse than this shared pity?

What could be better?

Judith bellowed internally. "Can you stop being so bloody soft and just find what you need to—?!"

"You don't get to order me around while we're the same person."

"I order myself around all the bloody time, you stupid woman!"

"We are going to have a talk about this, when . . . if I can get us home."

"What are you going to do about this one?" Judith mentally pointed to Rory, still curled up, holding on to the sprites like they were soft toys. "He's in your power now."

"So I can't just save you and the . . . sprites?" She'd found what they were called inside Judith's knowledge. She hadn't wanted to think that harsh a thought, but there were no barriers between the two women now.

"Oh, don't lie to yourself when someone's sharing

your brain. You won't leave him here to be crushed."

"I just wanted him to know I had the option. I'm in his head too."

Rory looked up, suddenly furious. "Get out!" he bellowed. "Don't touch me!" And he started to scream every epithet he knew. Everything about race, everything about gender, everything about anything he was not.

There was a long pause. Then, without another word inside Judith's head, something changed.

———————

The three fairies had suddenly reacted to something Lizzie didn't understand. As one, they'd shouted something guttural, and crouched. Then they had charged.

Lizzie hadn't hesitated. She'd grabbed the nearest kid and shoved them at the point where she'd encountered the anomaly, praying fervently as she did so, trying to push emotion into the act of pushing physically. The kid went straight past the anomalous space, and so Lizzie shoved her hands into it, calling out to anyone and anything who could help her in that instant, giving all her emotion to that in a way which she was used to in prayer.

She didn't have more than a moment. Then she'd have to get herself between the others, who were already starting to scream, run, push forward, and the danger that was coming for them. She'd wave her arms and try to look powerful, she decided. Oh God, she was going to die here.

"It's okay, Lizzie, I see you now!" a familiar voice shouted. In the centre of her own head. Kind of where she was used to God being. "Thanks for calling me. The fairies had put some sort of . . . curtain . . . in the way."

"Autumn?!" said Lizzie, boggled.

But in that second the shadows of the fairies hit them all, and the screams of panic turned to sheer terror, as Lizzie felt rather than saw the swing of three swords—

———

The swords passed over her.

And the others.

Lizzie felt a great sense of closeness to her old friend as they fell into darkness together, a voice and an intimate presence in her head, an astonishing embrace.

And then they were all standing there in the woods above Lychford on a late summer afternoon. Lizzie looked round and was relieved to see Judith, and Autumn, and with them Rory Holt, looking round, yelling as if he'd just been struck, and a man with a splint on his leg who was blinking, stunned, slowly getting to his feet, and all the ravers, and the DJ, and the lad who'd hugged her, and Stewie, and his bouncers, and half their generator, which was steaming and sparking where it had been cut in two, and no sign at all of the barn, which was now presumably lost somewhere in the great beyond along with the DJ's equipment . . . and floating in the air, a group of . . . perfect, smiling, giggling cherubs.

Rory Holt looked up at the creatures and broke into a gap-toothed grin. "That's what they really were," he said. "Little angels. They must have saved us."

Judith looked awkwardly at the other two. "Cherubs," she whispered out of the corner of her mouth. "Sprites, cherubs, I knew t'were one or t'other."

Autumn nodded in the direction of the cherubs, looking pointedly at Rory. "It looks like we brought some refugees over the border."

"What are you talking about?" He looked angry at her. "What have they got to do with that? They're little angels."

Lizzie found herself remembering certain lines from scripture about the need to treat strangers as if they might be angels.

Autumn's voice stayed calm as she addressed him again. "But you have me to thank."

Lizzie looked to Judith, but the old woman now had her hands stuck deep in the pockets of her cardigan, her expression unreadable, her body language saying she was deliberately taking no action.

"To thank for what? You got me into whatever that was. Probably drugs in my pint or summat. I'm going to tell the police." He looked fearful for a moment, as if Autumn might attack him. Then, reasonably certain he could turn his back on her, he started off down the hill, looking back over his shoulder from time to time, an expression on his face of valiant, infringed dignity.

"What an enormous wanker," said Stewie. And, thought Lizzie, he should know. She looked around at the kids from the rave. They were a mixture of angry and uncomprehending. They, like her, must all have had Autumn in their heads, and knew what she'd done. To them, that was all that mattered.

She turned back to see that Judith was watching Autumn to see what she would do next. Lizzie saw that the younger witch was holding in her hand something that Lizzie could only dimly see, a handful of glowing thread. "I can do maybe one more thing with this," she said.

"You could send him back," said Judith.

"But then," said Autumn, "the cherubs wouldn't get to go home."

And she opened her hand. In a blur of motion like released elastic, the cherubs vanished.

The man with the splint put a hand on Autumn's shoulder. "Good witch," he said.

Autumn turned to look at him with an expression which said she still wasn't sure.

———————

When the human witch had burst into the knot at the centre of the worlds, the shardling had seen the path home and seized its moment.

It had been relieved to take three steps and then find itself once again where it had been conceived, inside the long shadow that had fallen across the barrow of the court of the fairy king.

It relaxed. It had completed its mission.

It had been one of many sent out to map the disturbances of the boundaries, to swiftly bring back the information the king needed, now he was in the shadow, the information that would lead to war.

Because in the moment before it had left, it had seen the witch build a simple, single boundary. It was nothing like what had been there before. It would be easy to breach. The shardling felt a moment of satisfaction at having this information to return to its master.

The mind of the shardling only lasted for a moment longer before the king reached out and absorbed it back into himself. The knowledge was shared. The moment of satisfaction became a moment of anticipation.

The preparations for the attack began.

---

As the bells of the church chimed six, Autumn slowly and carefully unlocked the door of her magic shop, her two friends beside her. She felt like a different person from who she'd been the last time she was here, that morning.

Marcin had hugged her, and had thanked her profusely in English and Polish, had shown her a picture of his family, who she now felt she knew really well, having already experienced them inside his head. Now he could return to them. Even though . . . he'd made steering wheel gestures and Autumn had had to take a while to explain that his lorry was still lying there now, miles from the road in the real woods, the moment of time it had been trapped in having expired. It hadn't been left in fairy like the barn had been. Autumn felt dimly that she'd managed to arrange that on her way out of the structure of threads. Judith had got Lizzie to call Shaun on her mobile, and had taken the phone from her and sternly told her son that the lorry driver had been found and fought off some hijackers, heroically getting injured in the process. Apparently they'd used a helicopter to lift the . . . no, she'd interrupted his incredulous outburst, this was one of her sort of things, and so was Rory Holt, who was alive and well and would by now be back at his house and ready to tell a story that nobody would or should believe, and all the ravers were fine too, and did he have any more damn fool questions?

So Marcin, to Autumn's relief, had been able to go on his way with a reasonable future ahead of him. Result.

They sat down at the table in Autumn's workroom. Which was now clean, she realised, with nothing boiling itself on the stove. "Thank you," she said to Judith, now feeling unable to look at her. The old witch must have given some of her remaining energy to do that.

"Thank *you*," Judith replied, as though the words were from a foreign language.

"Well," said Lizzie, "this is better."

"Isn't anyone," said Judith, "going to make some bloody tea?"

———

So Lizzie made the tea. And listened, as she did so, to Judith and Autumn continuing to thank and apologise to each other, like nations who'd been at war and didn't quite know why. That was always, in her experience, the most wonderful sound. Judith was still an employee, Autumn still an apprentice, and who'd ever thought otherwise? Judith wanted to emphasise, Autumn having seen inside her head, that she'd been in her right mind when she'd voted, but no, she still wouldn't say which way that'd been. If Autumn didn't know already. Then Autumn, having moved swiftly past that, in whispers, was trying to persuade Judith to tell Lizzie something, but Judith was hesitant. That was okay. From the glimpse Lizzie had got inside her friend's head, she could guess what sort of thing this might be.

She put the mugs and teapot and a packet of Hobnobs down between them and decided to ask about wider issues. "What about all the people who now know about magic?"

"Nobody's going to believe those kids," said Judith, "and the smart ones won't try to tell anyone. Same for the lorry driver. He seems to know which side his bread's buttered. Rory Holt's going to tell everyone, for the rest of his days, and nobody will believe him, which sounds like the world's worked out a curse for him. Surprising how often there are just desserts."

"Or not," said Lizzie. "Can we find out what's happening in fairy?"

"I'll send messages to Finn," said Autumn. "I'm worried about him. What happened to you isn't something he'd have been up for, if he knew about it."

"If he could stop it," said Judith. "It wouldn't be the

first time there have been ructions in fairy. If they war on each other, we'll know about it. So will the world if we're not careful."

Lizzie went to point three on her short mental list. "And what are we going to do about the boundaries?"

"I tried to build a very rough one," said Autumn. "Okay, let's say it out loud, I ended up building a bloody wall."

Judith actually chuckled. Autumn immediately looked angry again. Lizzie looked sharply at Judith. Her smile was as thin as the smile on a fish, but it looked genuine. "I hadn't thought of that," she said. "I didn't mean it was your just desserts. Well, maybe a bit."

"I don't want it," said Autumn, still clearly requiring some terms and conditions here. "I want a proper border that treats all these worlds with respect and works on a case-by-case basis. I mean it. Not joking."

"Well, this'll be up to you, won't it?" said Judith. "What you put up, with what we put in place, will hold until someone has a real go at it. But we can't leave it. And we can't wait until I've got my strength back." If, thought Lizzie, privately, she ever did. "So you two will have to sort out what you want and build it. Soon."

Autumn looked a bit taken aback. "Okay," she said. "Thanks for . . . trusting—"

"No, we've had too many thanks already," said Judith,

"soft, both of you. And of course I trust you to . . . listen, you've made me say it, 'cos I'm going to have to start saying a lot of things now. This was why you messing up like that hurt so much—"

Lizzie looked to Autumn, but she shook her head, she wanted to hear this.

"—you, girl, are my choice to continue when I'm gone. To be the wise woman of this town. You'll have help from the vicar here, and maybe others'll come along, but someone'll have to do the lifting, and it won't be me forever. You and your . . . science," she let the word slip out like it was sour, "maybe that's the shape of what's to come. And the give and take of someone your age, that room for mercy, that'll be needed too. I just need you to . . . to not fly off at every enormous wanker, to be strong enough to be looked at like you're odd for the long haul."

"I . . . think I'm qualified—" Autumn was trying hard not to cry, and failing.

"Now I've seen in your noggin I know that. I know that you had a head start with that. Oh my girl. My girl. I don't know how long I got left." And Judith had to put a hand over her mouth and close her eyes. But she left one hand on the table. Autumn and then Lizzie put theirs on top of hers. And they stayed like that for a long time.

# Acknowledgments

As well as my wonderful editor on all three of these books, Lee Harris, I'd like to thank Jaine Fenn and sensitivity reader Dee Mamora, who's given me excellent insights. Go find her on Twitter, you can hire her too!

# About the Author

© Lou Abercrombie, 2015

**PAUL CORNELL** is a writer of science fiction and fantasy in prose, comics, and television, one of only two people to be Hugo Award nominated for all three media. A *New York Times* #1 bestselling author, he's written *Doctor Who* for the BBC, *Wolverine* for Marvel, and *Batman and Robin* for DC. He's won the BSFA Award for his short fiction and an Eagle Award for his comics, and he shared in a Writers' Guild Award for his TV work.

# TOR·COM

**Science fiction. Fantasy. The universe.**

**And related subjects.**

\*

More than just a publisher's website, *Tor.com*

is a venue for **original fiction, comics,** and

**discussion** of the entire field of SF and fantasy,

in all media and from all sources. Visit our site

today—and join the conversation yourself.